I0633383

LAST CALL

A MARRIAGE OF CONVENIENCE ROMANCE

BRIDGES AND BITTERS
BOOK 4

LAINEY DAVIS

By Lainey Davis
Join my newsletter and never miss a new release!
laineydavis.com

© 2023 Lainey Davis
All rights reserved. No portion of this book may be reproduced in any form without permission from the publisher, except as permitted by U.S. copyright law.

This is a work of fiction. Names, characters, businesses, events and incidents are the products of the author's imagination. Any resemblance to actual persons, living or dead, or actual events is purely coincidental.

Many thanks to Arwen Davis, Madison Pleins, and Elizabeth Perry for editorial input.
Edited by The Meet Cute Editor, LLC
Cover by Creme Fraiche Design

Thank you for supporting
independent authors!

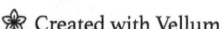 Created with Vellum

1

ESTHER

My stomach gurgles when I smell the peanut butter, but I know there isn't enough for me to indulge. I can grab something at work. I line up eight slices of bread, spreading the bread butts across two sandwiches. Later, when I cut them, I'll make sure each of my sisters has one butt, and hopefully nobody will argue about it. There's just enough jelly left for four good swipes.

The sandwiches are thin, but I think they'll do the trick. It's a lousy dinner for a bunch of young girls, but it's what we've got right now. Once I get paid tonight, I can stock up on some more stuff and keep it at my place. The girls can eat dinner at my apartment.

I leave a quick note for Eliza to make sure she grabs the SNAP card from Mom's wallet. The bar where I work is closed on Monday, so I can take her shopping with me after school and show her the best bargains. Someday, I won't have to come over here and look out for them.

As I walk to the bus stop, it occurs to me that I never even yell at our mother to do basic stuff like buy groceries for her daughters or make sure their school uniforms fit. When did I stop expecting that from her, I wonder?

It's not like it matters. The reality is I'm the responsible adult in my sisters' lives. Sometimes I consider fighting for legal custody of them, but I'm 25 and I'm as close to being able to hire a lawyer as I am to hiring a private chef. We'll make do.

THE CAGE IS PRETTY dead when I arrive. The boilermaker guys must have cleared out after their shifts ended, and the college kids won't show up until later. It's just me and Tony for now, minding our business as we each clean our respective areas. I hate that the morning shift leaves the bar all sticky and doesn't run the pint glasses through the dishwasher.

"Way to up the standard, Grace," I yell as she stomps out of the front door. She flips me off over one shoulder as she lights up a cig.

I stare out the front window at the French bakery across the street. I could sling macarons for a higher hourly wage in a clean, well-lit shop. Maybe my co-workers would smile at me. Maybe the patrons would be the kind who never look down my top or try to pinch my ass.

But a French bakery would probably have less flexibility if I needed to run to Rite Aid for emergency lice shampoo.

The tips are pretty good here at the Cage, and I like talking to the customers. Most of them. The college kids who come here tend to be paying their own way, but I like hearing about their big plans to change the world. The union guys who come here have families at home, and I like hearing them talk about showing up for their kids' baseball games.

There's a lot to love about tending bar.

"Esther, I'm going out for a smoke!" Tony hollers from the back as he sneaks into the alley. I wave a hand in the air to acknowledge him as I slam the dishwasher shut and begin prep for happy hour.

The clientele here like lite beer and well drinks, straight up. But every now and then, I can convince someone to let me fix them something special. Sometimes one of those pie-eyed college kids is celebrating an internship, and I whip them up a fizzy drink with unexpected garnish.

Sometimes Tony messes up someone's fruit salad, and I turn it into sangria that we drink together after last call.

It's a good job, overall. I learn a lot about people. I get laid when I feel like it.

My phone buzzes in my back pocket, and I fish it out to see a blurry photo of my sisters smiling around the plate of sandwiches I left for them. I see Eva has already gotten jelly on the collar of her school uniform. I'll try to remember to take some seltzer home later to help with the stain.

I hear the door to the bar open, and I slide my phone into my pocket as quickly as I pulled it out. It's a gang of guys in polo shirts and cargo shorts who look ready for cheap beer. I toss four napkins on the bar and flash them a fake smile. "What'll it be, boys?"

2

KOA

I drop my bag on the tile floor, and the sound echoes through the empty walls. This is it, the last look at my parents' house before the new owners walk through and sign the papers.

They better sign the papers. It took ages to sift through all the knickknacks, socks, cooking pots, and my mum's entire drawer full of erasers. For a pair of professed world travelers, they managed to accumulate entirely too much crap.

If I'm honest, it took ages because I went through it all bit by bit, until it started to get really painful. Then, I donated almost all of it. I can't hang on to any more than I can fit in a storage pod, since I have no idea how much longer I'll be able to stay in my flat.

It's been a month since my college advisor pulled me aside and insisted I face the facts: I have a paperwork problem. My parents put off dealing with my citizenship papers when they moved here for work, and then they died right after I turned 18.

As a college student, I had four years to work out the

details before graduation delivered both a diploma and an expired visa. At the time, I delayed the work out of spite. Obviously, that tactic didn't work very well for me.

I take one last look around the house, shake my head, and snap off the lights. I wonder, briefly, that I never got round to thinking of this as my house. It's always been *theirs,* but that's always meant I haven't had a place to call home.

Mum and Dad pulled me away from Aukland when I was 13 to come here and launch new programs in global studies, whatever that means. A Māori woman and her Pākehā husband dragging their only son across the world... only to die five years later.

I say New Zealand is home...but I don't know that it really feels that way to me. How many of my memories of Aotearoa are real, and how many are fairytales I've created? I hoist the tote bag of the last of my parental mementos onto my shoulder and set off on foot for the nearest dive bar.

I can afford swanky watering holes now thanks to inheritance and investments I don't know what to do with. But I prefer to blend into the background of a seedier spot. As much as a giant brown dude can blend in Pittsburgh.

I always stick out either because of my accent or my skin color. I suspect if I ever did go back to New Zealand, I'd even stick out there for being too American. I can't remember ever feeling like I fit in.

Mercifully, when I push through the door of the Cage, it's a ghost town. No sports on TV, no fried food special. Just me and this cracked pleather bar stool. "I'll take a pitcher," I say to the barkeep without glancing up.

And then I glance.

And then I keep on staring.

"Hey, there, pet," I say, leaning on my accent as I try to reverse course. This woman is gorgeous, with lush curves, tight jeans, and enough dark hair to cover my torso if she were on top of me. I'd like her to be on top of me.

"Not your pet." She slams the plastic pitcher in front of me with a splash and moves down the bar to wash a few glasses. I pour myself a cup of terrible beer and watch her. She'd be a terrific distraction from the mess of my paperwork situation.

"Like what you see?" She arches a brow when she catches me staring, but I don't look away.

"Yeah," I say, "Things are looking pretty good from where I'm sitting."

After nearly a decade in the States, I know my Kiwi lingo has faded a bit, but I can still amp it up when I try. She doesn't comment on my accent like most girls in this country, doesn't flutter her lashes and ask where I'm from. She doesn't say anything at all while she keeps herself busy cleaning and organizing, tidying stacks of cash from the register, and pocketing the tip jar stash.

I look over my shoulder and confirm I am definitely the only patron. Is she here alone in a dive bar after midnight?

"Tony's in the kitchen, and I'm pretty good with a blunt object, so don't get any ideas."

I hold my hands up. "My ideas were simply concern for your safety. Glad you've got Tony here." It's a lie. I hate Tony, whoever he is. I hate his proximity to this woman and how her lips form his name. I'm never jealous. You'd have to feel attached to be jealous, and yet something about this woman stirs up an urge in me.

I lean my elbows on the bar and take a sip of my beer. "I'm Koa."

"Mmm." She carries a tray of dirty dishes toward the back and kicks open the swinging door, emerging a few seconds later with a bar towel between her hands. I give her my best smile. "Still here, Koa?"

My grin stretches even further hearing her say my name. "Yeah. Gotta finish this pitcher, don't I?"

She leans forward to look at my progress. "Well, you've got a half hour. Better get to it."

I hadn't realized it was quite this late, but I'm in no mood to rush. Slowly sipping watery beer while I stare at this gorgeous bartender beats dragging my bag of memories back to an empty apartment. She's got curves for days, long dark hair, and icy blue eyes that seem like they've seen a thing or two. I take a swig. "Aren't bartenders usually quite talkative?"

She puts a hand on one hip. "You gonna tip me more if I tell you I like your eyes?"

That draws a laugh from me, and I slap a twenty on the bar. She yanks it away, opens the till, and raises another brow at me as she counts out the change. "You can keep it all if you tell me your name."

"How much is mine if I tell you to mind your own business?"

I shrug. "All of it, I guess. Can I tell you a secret?"

She sets her elbows on the counter. "They all do, sweetheart. They all do."

I set my cup down and inch closer. "Well, at the risk of being boring, I hate tipping. Loathe it. You shouldn't have to be nice to me for money."

"Koa, I haven't been nice to you at all."

"You remembered my name, though. We're making progress."

She busies herself a bit more, and I sip my drink, biding my time. "So where do you come from, that there's no tipping?"

"You looking to make a move?" She shrugs. I smile. "New Zealand," I tell her. "We...they pay people a living wage there." I can hear my father's voice as mine forms the words, and I shudder. Those are his sentiments, and he's not here.

She sniffs. "Must be nice."

I sigh. "I wouldn't really know. Haven't been back since I was young."

"Hm. Well, I haven't been anywhere since I was young, so I guess we have that in common."

"Maybe someday we'll go to the North Island together and not tip the barkeep."

"Hm." She's constantly in motion, wiping surfaces and organizing pens. I'm about to accept defeat and leave, but she says, "It's not a bad idea—paying the staff enough that they don't depend on tips."

"Want me to tell your manager to give you a raise?"

She laughs. "You're welcome to try." She looks at the clock, shrugs, and grabs a plastic cup from the stack by the register. "Do you really like that crap? I can make you something better..." She meets my eyes and I slide the pitcher toward her. I love how she dumps out the shitty beer and starts moving around the bar.

"You seem like a rum guy," she says, reaching for a bottle.

"Are you confusing me for a Jamaican?" I cross my arms over my chest, teasing.

She shakes her head and pulls a notebook from her pocket. "I can just tell. You probably like your drinks just that little bit sweet."

Just that little bit, my mother used to say when she'd dole out the toffee after supper. I swallow a lump in my throat and nod, unable to express the feeling that this woman somehow knew that about me. She mixes and pours, scribbles in her notebook, and slides it back in the pocket of her jeans.

She holds out a plastic cup, which I take. "Esther. My name's Esther."

I raise my cup to her, and she taps her own against it. We both drink, and my brows shoot up. The concoction is sweet and subtle, smooth and damn delicious. "Tell me more about your ideas, Esther. You gonna manage this place and pay the staff better?"

She shakes her head and wipes her mouth with the back of her hand. "Not this place, no." She bites her lip, like she's already said too much, but then decides to plow ahead. "Someday I'll have my own spot, though. And I will pay a living wage, and I'll charge accordingly for the drinks."

A thought occurs to me as she talks about wanting her own place, and I peer at her left hand in curiosity. No ring.

"So...I might not be here to visit your swanky new bar where you can be a smart mouth and still pay the rent."

"Ah, but I'm going to own the building." She smiles, dreamily. "No rent for me." We both laugh. I wait a beat, and she asks, "Where you heading that you'll miss my grand opening?"

"The thing is, Esther, I've overstayed my welcome here."

"At the Cage? Nah. You've got another ten minutes."

I shake my head. "Here, like...America."

She frowns. "They kicking you out? Did you try to *steal* someone's job?" She uses finger quotes when she says steal. "Stupid stereotype."

I wag a finger at her. "Cheeky, but no. I just, uh, don't have permission to stay here anymore."

I wait for her to ask me more questions, to indicate in some way that she wants to hear all about my parents dying before we dealt with my citizenship, how I coasted through university as a guest in the country I called home for a decade with no real connections to the land I left behind.

How I don't really fit in here but feel like this is where my only family sort of settled, and I don't know where else to go.

Esther doesn't ask, so I just say, "I've got a proposition for you."

She crosses her arms over her chest and rests against the register. From deep in the kitchen comes a bellow. "Esther! Lock up when you're done. I'm out."

"See you, Tony!" She doesn't turn her gaze from mine, nonplussed by the interruption. "Well?"

3

ESTHER

I half expect him not to show up at the courthouse.

I must have been delirious when I told Koa Stewart I'd marry him in exchange for the down payment on my own bar.

But just the thought of it fills me with warmth. My own business, where I control the profit, where I control everything. No more waiting for other people to make decisions, no more reacting. I can build up a nest egg, make sure my sisters have health care and shoes that fit.

"This is absolutely bananas," I mumble, tugging at my turtleneck collar as I look around the lobby. I check my phone again. No new messages since the last time he confirmed he'd be paying for everything but needed to stop to get cash from an undisclosed location. I saw his financial statements—I know he's good for the money. I also know he is on borrowed time here and has to be careful not to flag any authorities. Apparently, I'm getting the proceeds from the sale of his parents' house, before it ever hits his accounts.

I didn't bother to ask him why he doesn't just go to a bank. From what he said, he needs to lay low, so nobody notifies immigration that he finished college and is now roaming the streets of Pittsburgh as an undocumented menace to our social order.

I've spent the entire week irritated that there's nothing official he can do to stay here, other than marry an American. He moved here with his parents as a kid, and they were the ones who forgot to file all the papers so he could stay.

I clearly know nothing about rich people and how they live, other than the fact that they can't be bothered to deal with their kid's citizenship. It doesn't feel so different from poor parents who can't be bothered to get their kids health insurance.

While I might not understand the desire to stay if he has the option to leave, I can definitely appreciate that it sucks he has no choice in the matter.

After his indecent proposal, we sat at the bar well past closing time hashing out the specifics: we get married, he gives me a pile of money, I open the bar, and he rides off into the sunset to coach rugby...somewhere. It all sounded so simple. We used my phone to apply for a marriage license on a county website so bad that I wanted to stop paying taxes on principle. Not that I ever earn enough to owe taxes. But I will once we do this thing. I will be middle class, damn it.

But then I didn't hear a word from him for three days. Three entire days wondering if the whole thing was a dream. Three days of me searching for him online and finding his obnoxiously happy face everywhere, arms draped around teammates. Shirtless and sweaty...the man is disruptive.

"A richer-than-sin disruption," I mutter, and then I see him. All six-foot-something of muscle and tan skin. Beaming, of course. "Thought you weren't coming," I say, and then I flush because I notice he's carrying a pale purple rose along with a thick envelope.

"Could have said the same," he says, sliding the cash into my bag and leaning toward me. "But we have a bargain, and I always keep my word."

I swallow, not used to people doing so. "Me, too," I stammer. "I keep my word."

He smiles like he was born doing it--maybe he was. Or maybe he's just happy to be dealing with his problems. "For you, my bride." He presents me with the flower and winks. "Shall we?"

I shrug, and we get in line, ignoring the fact that my legs are threatening to melt. I don't do things like swoon or melt for charming men. I sniff the rose without thinking, inhaling the rich scent. People don't give me things, not small things like a flower and not big things like the key to my dreams.

People are more likely to give me strep throat than flowers. I just had my youngest sister at Urgent Care for a strep test. I start to wonder if my throat is scratchy or if I'm just parched. I can't get sick, can't afford to take days off, so I will my body to produce more saliva.

Koa watches me sniff the flower, and I jerk it down to my waist, away from my nose. The scent lingers, and I bite my lip, a bad habit I can't seem to quit. "Tell me again why your parents didn't deal with your visa?"

He rolls his eyes. "You'd think a couple of uni professors would know better. I guess it's like how the cobbler's children have no shoes."

"The cobbler's children? Are we elves, Koa? Are there still cobblers in New Zealand?"

He puts his weight against the wall, smirking. "Chur, bro. There were last time I checked."

Before I can think of a return quip, the grumpy clerk makes eyes at us, her entire expression communicating, "Get on with it. I'm busy." I like her immediately.

"We're here for the judge." Koa's words emerge slowly, his accent a little thicker than it is in conversation with me. "It's our wedding day."

I smile, hoping it seems believable. I wish he wouldn't sling around terms like "wedding," as if this weren't a paper-work situation.

A business deal.

Like marriages in old timey romance books, ours will be in name only, and we plan to live separate lives. As soon as Koa gets his Green Card, we can file for divorce. I had to stifle a laugh when he seemed so anxious, worried I'd want to remarry and feel burdened by our arrangement. As if I would ever have time to be someone's wife!

I smile again as Koa rubs my arm. I have no idea how long it will take for him to actually get the Green Card that lets him stay in this country, but hopefully sooner than later. I want the *bar* to be the thing I add to my responsibility list —not a husband.

I glance away from staring at his ass in his khaki slacks, because the last thing I want to do is catch feelings for my sort-of-husband. Even if those feelings are just the lusty variety. Better to keep things uncomplicated.

My phone buzzes in my pocket, and I turn it to airplane mode. My sisters can wait a half hour.

Koa places an arm around my shoulder to steer me down the hall toward the elevator. I stiffen initially—but I remember that Koa and I are supposed to be madly in love, and there's something soothing about the strum of his fingers on my shoulder, where he taps a rhythm while we wait.

He takes my hand once we're on the proper floor, and we walk together into the tiny office that's not at all what I imagined a judge's chambers would look like. The old, bespectacled man behind the desk is wearing a robe, though, so I take a deep breath and stride ahead, clutching the rose in one hand and Koa's thick fingers in the other. He slides our paperwork across the desk and, after a few blurry minutes I won't remember, the deed is done.

I stare at the stamped form and think about all it represents. Security for me and for my sisters. A future, a real opportunity to own a business. All I have to do is lie and pretend I'm in love with this man.

Honestly, I do love that he's helping me transform my life. And that's enough for my conscience. I just hope it's enough for immigration. We have a whole plan worked out where he's going to send me postcards from his travels. He's not going to have a regular address, so I agreed to periodic, loving emails.

I can send a loving email. I'm sure of it.

"What should we do to celebrate, Wife?" Koa's mouth is close to my ear as we stand outside waiting for the light to change.

I turn to glance at him. "Um...head to the bank?" I'm only half joking, but his face falls a little, and I can tell he was expecting me to have at least a little bit of fun with this successful arrangement. "Get you some health insurance?" I try to add a smile to this last bit and lighten the mood I fear I've spoiled.

"You're really worried I'm going to keel over?"

I flail my arms. "You could break an ankle or fall in a sink hole. You just never know. I say we sit down and apply for some bennies with our dollars."

He sighs. "How about we find some lunch at least. Where do you like best?"

"Nicky's Thai," I blurt, without thinking. The tiny place near my apartment is full of plants, so it feels like I could be in Thailand. It's also cheap and delicious.

Koa taps around on his phone and nods, then surprises me by striding toward a motorcycle parked near the court-house. I take in the scene as he opens a bag and pulls out a dark helmet. His tan-skinned hand shines beneath the cuff of his button-down shirt, and I realize he dressed up for our ceremony. I wore jeans and a turtleneck...I fidget with my rose and pull my purse tighter against my side.

I normally would be all over a motorcycle ride with a sexy stranger, but I'm not sure why I hesitate as Koa gestures for me to take the helmet. I'm so flustered and surprised that I drop the rose he gave me. I just stand there looking weird while it flutters to the sidewalk.

Koa bends to pick it up and brushes a bit of dried leaf from the silken petals. He tucks the rose behind my ear and then gently settles the helmet onto my head. I climb onto the bike behind him, wrap my arms around his solid waist, and wonder what the hell I just got myself into.

Kia ora, babe! Made it to San Fran. Weath-

er's pretty bleak. Thought you'd like this pic of
the seals. I feel like that big fella in the
middle after a week on my bum, driving. Going
to meet the lads soon. Take care.

    Koa

FROM: Esther Storm

    To: Koa Stewart

    Subject: Great

Hey. Got your postcard. Did you also send chocolate? It was really good. My sisters all agree it's way better than the Hershey stuff here in PA.

I quit the Cage the other day and found a spot of my own. I decided I'm going to call it Bridges and Bitters. Cute, right?

It's sort of near the 40th Street bridge, and I'm plenty bitter.

I think I'm going to add that drink I made you to my menu. Maybe it'll be my very first special...

Talk to you soon, I hope.

~Esther

To my darling wife,
    I can't believe I get to spend a season here
in Key West. You wouldn't believe the number of

cats prowling about. If you were here, we could go out and pet pussies together.

Remind me your shoe size, and I'll send you some sandals. A lot of the lads work in the factory when they're not training with me. Proper cobblers, eh? Cool as.

There's so much rum down here, too. Think of me when you drink some, eh?

xoxo Koa

FROM: Esther Storm

To: Koa Stewart

Subject: Re: Re: Re: Re: Re: Re: Re: Great

Did I tell you my mom didn't even show up for Eila's graduation? I feel like all I do is bitch to you about her, but it's not like there's anyone else I can say this stuff to. I took a million pictures. Let me tell you, I worked hard to put a smile on my face for them. I was steaming mad. I felt like that caldera from the postcard you sent. Where was that? Wyoming? Maybe my mom is there...she sure as hell isn't here.

Anyway, things at the bar are amazing. I'm operating in the black. I learned that phrase in my business class at the community college. I'm sure my mother would skip that graduation, too, if I told her it was happening.

I funneled my feelings into a new cocktail. I'm calling it Purple Rage. It's got bourbon, plum syrup, lemon juice, creme de violette, lavender bitters, a plum garnish, and all my frustration.

I'm charging twice what I normally would, and you know what? It's moving like lightning.

Take that!

~Esther

4

ESTHER

Another one-night stand, another reminder that they're not worth it.

I look over at the woman in my bed with a blissful expression on her sleeping face, but I feel nothing.

Each time, it's like I'm trying to scratch an itch, but the relief is so short-lived. They get off. I get off. And then I still have the same responsibilities. The same worries. The same endless to-do list.

I have to stop these one-night stands.

I also have to get to work. We've got an event tonight at my bar.

I still love the sound and feel of those words even after five years: my bar. Mine.

Has it really been that long since that day I got married, got tipsy, and had an ill-advised night in the sack with my fake husband? I try not to think about that part. Clearly, I've been trying to quit the one-night stands for a long time.

My phone starts to ping, telling me the do-not-disturb period has ended. I glance through the list quickly, scroll past the social texts, and quickly respond to each of my sisters' questions.

> Baking soda is different than baking powder.

> Try some cranberry juice if it's burning, Eden.

> All your birth certificates and social security cards are here at the house in a fire safe. Just tell me when you need a photocopy.

Not too taxing in the scheme of things. I stretch with a groan, trying to wake up...what's her name even? Was it Sara? I feel like everyone is named Sara these days.

She rolls toward me and cuddles against my side, and I realize this is going to be uncomfortable. "Hey," I say, a few decibels beyond a whisper. "We gotta move."

"Mmmmm," she groans, smiling even bigger. "Too early."

I give her a gentle shove as I back out of the bed on my side, kicking off the covers. "I'm serious. I have to work."

She doesn't open her eyes. "It's Saturday..."

"Yes." I yank the covers all the way off the bed, and she gasps, curling into a ball against the chill. "And I own a bar. Sooo...."

I drift off and cross my arms over my chest as she huffs and searches the floor for her clothes. "I thought we'd be able to get brunch."

I sigh. "I thought I was clear that last night was...just last night." To be honest, I'm usually surprised when the people I bring home from a bar think that we are doing anything more than getting our rocks off. I mean...we met at a bar.

A nice bar! But this was a bar hookup. It's not like I

habitually seek out my patrons for sex, but when I go home with one, I never sugarcoat anything.

I grab a robe from the hook by the door and belt it as my guest tries to get dressed. I'm not going to be able to shower until I walk her all the way to the door. I can tell.

And she's probably going to want some goodbye comfort, try to give me her number. She bites her lip after tugging on the slinky tank top that caught my eye the night before. I gave her extra cherries in her Manhattan for that tank top. And then she did that trick with her tongue and the stem...

I briefly consider yanking her into the shower with me, but that would send a mixed message.

"So, this was fun." I smile. It was fun. I had fun. She had fun. Why is she hesitating?

She nods her head. "I just didn't think you'd have to go back in so early. Do you want to text me when you get done with your shift today?"

I shake my head. "It's not a shift. I own the bar. I'm there open to close. I'm sorry. I just don't have time for anything substantial." I pause and her lip wobbles. "I meant it when I said all that last night."

Finally, resigned, she shrugs and walks toward the door. She waves, and I smile, closing the barrier between us gently as she backs down my front steps. At least she didn't scream and wake my sister. I can hear Eva snoring away, and I'm glad she will get enough rest.

I GET myself ready and head in to Bridges and Bitters, smiling as I always do when I unlock the front door and slip inside. Every single thing in this bar is my idea, from the decor to the drink menu. I chose each of the stools based on the height of their foot ring because I wanted my female patrons to be able to sit comfortably.

Inspired by the women who boldly drank in public during Prohibition, I gave the whole place a Speakeasy feel and then read up on cocktails from that era. But my bar isn't dark or tucked in a secret basement. I found a beautiful storefront on a busy street and bought the damn building.

The room smells like Pine-Sol and lemon cleanser, and I'm glad Eva made me let her close up last night so I could head on home with what's-her-name.

Everything is in perfect order right now, and I feel a tiny release of tension I'd been holding at trusting my kid sister to wash glasses and mop the floors. It's silly to insist on being the one to do that part of the job.

And then I remember that the real crucial task of closing involves the cash from the till, and I rush to my office to check the safe. I sigh in pleased relief when I see the bank bag, padlocked as instructed. Okay, maybe my sister is an actual adult capable of some basic bookkeeping and space maintenance. Noted.

It still feels too huge to let go of any control over this business. After all, it's here because I made a pretty risky bargain. I try not to think about what would happen if I lost this place. Sure, my sisters are all older now, but what about me? What the hell would I be without my own business?

I check the mailbox outside, hating how much I hope there's a postcard from *him*, but there's nothing there. It's been a while. I realize it's also been a while since I sent him an email, even to complain. For years, he's been this receptacle on the other end of the internet, someone I never have to see. Someone who doesn't ask a single thing from me. Gradually, I started spilling my guts to him. It's cathartic.

I HURRY through my orders for the coming week, sign for today's deliveries at the back, and refrain from flipping off the guys renting the building next door. They're always asking me to do things for them, and they're always trying to throw their garbage in my containers no matter how many times I explain that I pay for garbage and recycling services, and so should they. I only do things for people I care about. I do not do things for entitled men running fake laundromats with no washing machines.

Before long, the caterers arrive with the supplies for the book launch party I'm hosting today. Knowing my preference to support women in business, my friend Samantha recommended a place nearby, and they do a great job setting up linens and centerpieces for the booths and high-tops.

Sam, Chloe, and Piper are the core members of my friend group. It took me a really long time to admit that I have a friend group, so it's a big deal that I think of these gals in that way.

We call ourselves FOOF—fresh out of fucks. We meet in the back room here at Bridges and Bitters, talking about work and life and smashing the patriarchy. I love it, even if I'm usually floating in and out checking on my customers. I'm not ready to bare my soul to them, but every now and then I'll share something cool about the bar. Like when I won a people's choice award from the local newspaper. The wall plaque doesn't really match my speakeasy vibe, but I hung it in the hall near the bathroom.

We're celebrating Chloe's book launch today. She writes historical romance, so all the food and decor are period appropriate.

Chloe says so, anyway. I have no freaking clue what sorts of snacks people ate in the early 1800s, but I definitely know what drinks they would serve. I came up with The Scofflaw for this party, and it's damn good. I get started prepping it in batches, measuring out the rye whiskey, dry vermouth, lemon juice, and Grenadine before zesting some oranges into the mix.

"ESTHERRRRRR!" Sam's voice sings down the hall and into the event room, and I know the party is about to get lit.

"I'm back here, Sam. You're early." I fling a towel over my shoulder and smile, seeing her decked out in some sort of colonial wench outfit.

Her boyfriend, AJ, grins and hooks a thumb at Sam. "She tried to get me to wear jodhpurs. I said no."

"You look great, AJ." I kiss him on the cheek and pinch Sam's behind as I edge past them in the hall. "I gotta get the drinks going!"

Sam leans over the bar and watches me as I continue making batches of today's custom cocktail. "Esther, your knife skills are terrifying and admirable." Sam grabs a slice of orange from me before I start popping twists on the rims of the glasses.

I give her a wink and return to work as our other friends start to trickle in. I love that my friends are enthusiastic, but it makes me nervous when they come this early to a big event. I feel like I can't find any quiet space to go through mental checklists. Nothing to be done about it now, though.

I can handle this like I handle everything else.

I have a few staffers on weekends, and soon enough Ruthie rolls in with a smile. I relax a smidge. She steps behind the bar next to me, prepping signature drinks before the first rush of romance readers arrives. Soon, the party is in full swing. Chloe is glowing with happiness and her new audiobook narrator, Cash, is begrudgingly accepting praise from fans.

Before long, a stranger walks up to the bar for a drink. "What can I get ya?" I don't even look up, my hands flying as I pour another round of cocktails.

It's a guy this time, maybe here with a wife who loves Chloe's books. He scratches his chin, considering, and I ignore him while I attempt to get caught up on drink orders. Eventually, he asks, "You got any absinthe?" I sigh and shake my head. This is so clearly a whiskey-centric event.

"Come on," he drawls, leaning forward. "I'll pay extra."

"We're slammed, my dude. I've got all sorts of local spirits. You ever tried Maggie's Farm rum?"

He waves a hundred-dollar bill at me, and I roll my eyes, plunking a set of glasses on a tray. "Ruth, order up." I look at the guy and snatch the money from him. "Give me two seconds."

I hurry to the back closet for the lone case of absinthe. I only carry it at all because we have a local distillery in the neighborhood. I mostly use them for their gin. I snatch a bottle of the green fairy and head back to the bar, gesturing at the guy. I grab a glass and a perforated spoon, plunking a sugar cube in the middle.

Based on his surprised expression, he's not actually a regular drinker of the elixir, and I smile smugly as I drip cold water over the sugar. I'm about to hand it to him when I hear a voice I'm not expecting.

I look up, my hand frozen in the customer's palm, both of us gripping the glass. I see a smiling, tanned face and dark eyes crinkled in pleasure from beneath a curly mop of even darker hair.

"There you are, Wife." He winks, and I drop the spoon.

5

KOA

I bend to pick up the spoon and lean past the bar to toss it into the sink as Esther stares at me, eyes wide. Her customer looks annoyed to be kept waiting so I pluck his drink from my wife's hand and slide it along the wood, without looking away from her. "Place looks great," I say, meaning it.

She's come a long way from the sticky dive bar where we met. Hell, this place doesn't even smell like tobacco or stale beer. She remains frozen in place as I drink her in, and I take my time about it. The last time I saw her, she was asleep and naked, tangled in sheets on the floor of her flat while I snuck away.

Maybe it wasn't sneaking. That was our arrangement. Sign the papers, skip town. We never mentioned sex, and once I woke up with my wits, I felt like trash leaving her like that. Obviously not trash enough to call or apologize.

Seeing her now, I wonder how the hell I managed to walk away at all. Not only is she gorgeous, but she's assertive and an all-around boss. A total catch. But that's what I do, isn't it? I leave. Whether I'm a kid leaving my home country with my parents or a nomad chasing after the next job opening, I skip town before I form anything so dangerous as attachment.

It's been brutal holding back, keeping her in my mind as a pen pal even though our messages convey so much more than that. At least on my end. I told her we should build a stockpile of evidence that we're happily married. I've come to rely on that correspondence, though. And I'm old enough to know attachment never did me any favors.

A woman approaches me at the bar, her face skeptical. I ran into them in the hall, and I remember her boyfriend's red beard. Lousy bugger is coated in hair, and I can barely sprout a mustache.

"Esther, who is this guy?" The woman scowls at me as my estranged wife remains frozen stiff. Considering I probably caught the pair of them rooting in Esther's closet, I figure they don't have much of a leg to stand on. "I'm Piper." She turns toward me, trying another tack. "Who are you and how did you break Esther?"

I laugh. "She's not broken. She's just a wee bit beached as. I should have let her know I was coming."

"Beached as?" Piper wrinkles her nose, and I remember once more that I'm a stranger in this country. How could I forget?

Esther shakes herself, like she's snapping out of a fog. "Koa."

I grin, nodding. "The one and only." Noticing that Esther is definitely shaken up, I look around the bar. Surely after all these years, she wouldn't still be working alone behind the planks. Hell, there's not even a kitchen here to hide a surly line cook. "Can you step away for a few?"

Esther nods rapidly and looks around. Spotting another woman in jeans with a tray, Esther signals for her to pop behind the bar and takes a few wobbly steps down the hall. "Easy now." I skirt around Piper and the boyfriend, supporting Esther with my arm so she doesn't trip.

We reach the office, and Esther sinks into a chair, shaking her head while humming. "What the fuck, Koa?" Her shock seems to be melting away, revealing the feisty woman I remember marrying.

"I tried calling. Seems you changed your number."

Esther groans and drops her head into her hands, elbows digging into the top of the desk as her dark hair hides her face. "My stupid sisters."

I take a seat in the folding chair opposite her, only a wee bit concerned it'll buckle under my weight. I've bulked up a bit since I've had nothing better to do. "Right. Sisters. How many of them are there again? Four?" I know exactly how many sisters she has because I've memorized every word she's written me about them, about her mother, about this bar.

She nods. "I gave my phone to Eva when she graduated. My number now is the number for Bridges and Bitters."

I cross my arms over my chest. "Makes it pretty hard to leave work behind when you do it that way, pet."

That gets her to whip her head back up. "We talked about that. I'm not your pet."

I wink at her. "Nah, but you are my wife. And we have some marital business to discuss." I sigh and rake a hand through my hair. "Looks like the immigration folks finally caught up with their paperwork."

She frowns. "What's that mean? Are they kicking you out?" She flies to her feet, hands clenched in fists.

"Easy now. No, remember we have to do an interview? Prove we're mad for each other. That sort of thing."

"Didn't they already give you the paperwork to stay?"

I shake my head. "No, babe. That's all temporary. And time's up on that." I take a deep breath and smile. "We gotta prepare for our performance or else, face the music."

She arches a dark brow, and I want to fuck that look right off her face, smack her luscious behind, and feel her squirm around on my cock again. But somehow, I doubt we'll get a repeat performance of our wedding night. Esther made it very clear that was only due to her surprise that the Thai restaurant served alcohol at lunchtime.

I fish in my cargo shorts for the letter I got from immigration. "My beloved wife and I must report to the field office in two weeks."

Esther squints at the paper and then draws her head back in irritation. "That says Philadelphia. I live in Pittsburgh."

I shrug. "Looks like we're about to take a road trip then, doesn't it."

She starts shaking her head rapidly, and I try not to admire what that motion does to her breasts. It's been way too long since I stared at a proper pair of cans. "Koa, I don't take road trips. I don't just run off and leave the bar unattended. I'm running a business here."

Now it's my turn to recoil. "You don't have staff? Who'd you leave behind the bar just now?"

Esther throws her hands up. "I can't just leave my staff in *charge*, Koa."

"And why not?"

Esther stares at me for a long time before she stands and walks out of the room in a huff. My wife is deeply irritated by something I said about her refusal to take a holiday. I remember that we haven't actually spoken in years, that we've been performing all the pillow talk in our emails and cards. The thing is, seeing her now, competent and confident and gorgeous as all get-out...I find myself deeply turned on, and I vow to drag her away from here kicking and screaming until she agrees to relax.

6

ESTHER

"Did that man say husband?" Piper turns to Samantha and Chloe, who she's dragged up the hall to wait for me. "He said husband. I heard him refer to Esther as his wife."

I hold up a hand to my friends. "Look, guys. I can't deal with this now. Chloe, this is your party. This is about you today."

Chloe mashes her lips together and seems to vibrate as her gaze focuses on something behind me. I don't need to turn around to know it's Koa standing there, probably smirking. I feel the heat of his body as he steps closer to my back, and I close my eyes, trying to concentrate. "Right. I'm going back up front to sling drinks."

I ignore all of them for a bit, mixing a few more batches of today's signature cocktail. This party is about Chloe and her book release. Koa should respect that not everything is about him. He could have tried harder to contact me, could have sent a postcard.

And I would have told him to fuck off. Ugh, I'm so predictable. No wonder he showed up out of the blue. I risk a glance to where he's found a seat on a barstool. I look at his brown hands folded gently together on the bar, like he's patiently waiting for a meeting to start.

My husband-on-paper has beefed up since I saw him last. I try to banish thoughts of that night, of my wedding night. I hadn't intended to sleep with him, but he looked so damn good, and we drank so much rum at the Thai place. I start to sweat, remembering how he manhandled me in so many delicious ways against my door, on my creaky old futon, and eventually on the floor of my apartment.

I don't live in a rat hole apartment anymore. Our arrangement got me this business and the beautiful house in Manchester that I can welcome my sisters to when they need someplace to stay. I remind myself that Koa Stewart turned my life around and kept my family safe. I nod at him, which is the closest I can bring myself to a smile at the moment.

Eventually, the party dies down and most of the guests leave. The core Foof ladies stick around, of course. I sense the three of them lurking, shooing away their menfolk as if I'm going to give them all the dirt with Koa still sitting at the bar oozing sexiness.

Samantha, still decked out in colonial garb from the book party, smacks the wood of the bar. "Esther. I had no idea you were into dudes."

That shocks a laugh out of me, and I'm grateful she has the ability to break tension like this. Koa leans against the back of his stool, crossing his arms over his chest. "My wife is pan," he says proudly, his accent making it sound like he called me a pen. I do feel inky at the moment, dark.

I shrug, acknowledging his words, remembering how we hashed out the rules of our union: none, really. I told him from the outset that I'm not really into labels when it comes to sexuality. I've just always been attracted to everyone. And that's the setup we created. Fuck whoever we want. Live however we want. Only call if there's an emergency. And then I went and changed my number and forgot to update him.

"Guys, I need to kick you all out of here. You're scaring away the customers, and I can't afford to close up early on a Saturday night." It's a lie. I already budgeted for tonight to end when the book release party ended. I built that into the rental fee for the space. I just need them all to get the hell out of here so I can think. And, I suppose, have a conversation with my husband.

Piper squints at me and jabs my chest with her pointer finger. "You're not off the hook, Esther Storm. You're going to spill your guts to us as soon as you're done catching up with Mr. Muscles here."

Koa flexes his bicep and waggles his eyebrows at Piper, who laughs. "Let me know if you need a spot to work out while you're in town, Muscles."

"Name's Koa," he says, winking at her. "And that would be sweet as. Ta."

The three women sigh and head out the front door where I can see AJ, Teddy, and Cash waiting for them, trying not to press their faces to the glass windows in curiosity. I can tell I have a lot of explaining to do later.

I drop the bar towel from my shoulder onto the wood. "Where are you staying? Let's go talk."

He laughs long and hard, shaking his head. "Esther, aroha. You're my wife and we're due for an interview with immigration. Don't you think I should stay at yours?"

I purse my lips. I had not thought that far ahead. "I guess you're right. But I don't have a spare room right now. My sisters..."

I break off my train of thought as his grin widens. "Even better. I like to be the big spoon. Do you still have that crap mattress, or did you use your windfall for an upgrade?"

I roll my eyes at him and tip my chin toward the back door. "Come on. I'll show you my new digs."

Koa follows me home on his motorcycle, and I realize he doesn't know my address. He sends his postcards to the bar, sends paperwork to the bar when he needs to...I've really kept him in the dark about a lot of things. But damn it, I told him when I married him that I don't have it in me to care for anyone other than my sisters. I used up all my caregiver energy as a kid. I didn't ask to be the oldest sister, and none of us asked for a flakey mom or absent fathers.

Our mom is doing all right these days, but my sisters still come to me first whenever they need to know how to fake-hem a pair of pants or figure out which bus gets them home from downtown. They learned early that they can always rely on me, and I'm not about to let them down. Ever.

I decide not to turn left on a yellow light so Koa can keep up, not that I don't think his motorcycle is capable of zooming around traffic, but because I don't want him to risk getting pulled over...or harming himself. I should care about his well-being. I can spare that much energy.

I pull up in front of my house and smile at the brightly painted door, glowing pleasantly in the streetlights. He helped me get this place. I need to do better by him.

7

KOA

My wife upgraded from her shitty, smelly flat into a gorgeous house. From the outside, I'm not sure if it's one of those old Pittsburgh houses that was divided into multiple flats or if this is all one big home. As I watch her walk to the door, it's obvious there's one post box, one address. One giant household.

I don't bother to wonder if she filled it with babies or something like that. She's been clear from the start that she already did her share of parenting and isn't interested in kids. I park the bike and join her on the stoop, marveling at her plump lips in the dim light. I really want to dig my hands into that ass of hers again, but I tell myself that's just the lust and the nostalgia simmering.

"This is me," Esther says, fingers trailing along a metal sign by her door. STORM CHALET, it reads.

"That's clever." I tip my chin at the sign. "You're always clever." The faintest hint of a smile tips her lips as if she's trying to hide her pride for the home she's built. A gust of wind hits a set of chimes hanging from a hook in the tiny garden out front, and I watch her shiver. "Can we go in?"

"Oh, yes. Of course." Esther unlocks the door and gives it a shove, and I watch as lights flick on automatically. Not a brilliant deluge, but a gentle circle of warmth to help her in late at night. Another perfect touch for someone who keeps odd hours and, evidently, has other people at home she doesn't want to disturb. "My sister's asleep," Esther whispers.

I furrow my brow. "The one who likes goats?" She shakes her head. "That was Eliza. She's got her own place now. Eva is staying here for a bit."

"And who's in the other bedrooms?" At her puzzled glance, I remind her she suggested I sleep on the couch.

"Oh. Well." She shakes her head. "Come on. I'll give you a tour." She circles a hand at the living and dining rooms. "Self-explanatory. Kitchen's through there. There's never food in it."

She presses a finger to her cherry-red lips and heads up the stairs. I hoist my duffel over one shoulder and follow her, shrugging at her incredulous expression. The second floor of the house is a ring of doors, each with a cursive capital E painted in the center, except for one that's ajar and clearly houses the toilet.

"You keep rooms for each of them?" She lifts one shoulder. "But you wouldn't let your husband crash in one of the beds?"

Esther backs up the stairs to the third floor looking irritated. "Maybe if my husband gave me some notice, I could have checked with them." She flicks on the light at the top of the stairs to reveal a massive bedroom with open nooks full of clothes and shoes as well as a bathroom complete with a claw-foot tub. I hurry away a mental image of her lounging in there, luscious tits bobbing above the bubbles.

"Maybe if my wife gave me her phone number, I could

have given her notice." I cluck my tongue and drop my bag as Esther tucks herself into a little couch, folding her legs under her as she leans one arm across the back. She's gotten a tattoo since I saw her last, flowers and birds inked all badass on her forearm. There's an armchair nearby, but I wedge myself into the sofa next to her. "It matters, you know, that I can't reach you."

"Look," she says. "I wasn't expecting you. My sisters keep things in their rooms. They don't have another family home to store their childhood crap...it's important to me to create that for them."

I drop a hand to her leg and meet her glance. "I'm not here to shred the old report cards and swim trophies. Honest." She nods, and I smile, leaning back against the opposite arm of the couch. "So, catch me up, Wife. What have you done with our bargain since I saw you last?"

She snorts. "You know it all, Koa. I bought Bridges and Bitters, opened it, slayed at running it. I bought this house, fixed it, brought my sisters into it."

"Your mum still out of the picture?" I think of her confessing her dark secrets to me over email, and I know she doesn't share her frustrations with anyone else. I fight the urge to tug that kerchief from around her ponytail and unleash her dark mop of hair.

Esther shrugs. "Mom is stable right now. Not drinking as much. Still more invested in her bingo circuit than her kids." I nod as she stares at my arms. "What the hell have you been doing? You're massive."

I grin. "Oh, just enjoying my health insurance." She laughs. "I've been training with the lads I coach, here and there."

She frowns. "That's it? That can't possibly pay very well in this country."

I shake my head. "It doesn't. But I don't need money, do I? Got myself down to what fits on the bike, plus whatever's in the storage unit here. Thank you for looking after that, by the way."

"Koa, I literally never think about your storage unit. It's on auto pay. I probably didn't remember to give them an updated phone number, either..."

This time, I do let myself touch her hair. My fingers reach out to fiddle with the ends where they fall on her shoulders. "I'm sure it's all fine. Anyway, I didn't want to commit to anything long-term until I got my permanent leave to remain. Rugby teams are always looking for unemployed Kiwis."

"You just...wander around playing sports? With no possessions?"

I squint at her. "You telling me you couldn't live without 90 percent of the things in this house? I know you, Esther Storm. You don't care a fig about stuff."

She nods. "That's fair." Then she yawns. And keeps yawning. "I gotta get some sleep, Koa. Can we pick this conversation back up in the morning?" She nudges my leg with her foot. I stand up and watch in surprise as she gives a quick push to the back of the couch, flipping it down to form a bed. "There's pillows and blankets on that shelf." She points as she walks toward the bathroom. By the time I help myself to a few things, she's out of the bathroom, nestled into her massive bed, and snoring softly as her tattooed arm dangles off the side.

I turn off the lights and lie down, staring at her in the glow of the streetlamp through the window. Even on a shitty fold-out bed I feel at home here. Or...welcome, at least. I fall asleep with a smile on my face.

8

ESTHER

My house smells like food. Someone is cooking.

Maybe I'm about to have a seizure or something...I swear my friend Emma told me she smells weird food before she has a seizure. There isn't food at my house unless Eva went grocery shopping. Fat chance.

I sit up in bed, remembering that Eva isn't the only person under my roof right now. I have so much explaining to do. I told my friends I made a business deal when I got the money for the bar, but never went into the specifics. They don't know the deal involved a man.

Koa.

I glance at the pull-out bed, which has been neatly made. His bag is arranged next to his pillow, all zipped up and tidy. I toss on my robe and pad down to the first floor, the smell of bacon and onions drawing me to the kitchen.

I freeze in the doorway as my estranged husband shakes a skillet over the gas flame while my sister stares at him, dreamily, with her chin resting on her palm.

Neither of them notices me and they continue a conversation I've walked in on.

"So, after my folks died, I was able to stay on at university with a student visa. I finished my degree, and now..." Koa shrugs and gives the pan a firm shake. "Now I'm hanging out with your sister, I guess." He turns to dump some food on a serving plate on the island and sees me. "Hello, gorgeous." He winks and then spins back to shut off the burner. "Just in time."

Eva and I remain motionless as Koa plates the food. There are scrambled eggs, buttered toast, bacon, and... "Are those beans?"

I drag out a stool and sit, staring at my plate. Koa has already begun eating his, and I notice he's shoveled the beans on top of his bread. "Oh yeah. Beans on toast is the bomb. Did I get that right, Evie?"

My sister nods and dutifully shovels her own beans on top of the bread. I eye them skeptically but begin to eat. The food is greasy and filling and perfect after a full day on my feet yesterday, paired with the shock of my past showing up in town. I notice that my sister doesn't correct Koa's nickname for her, and I arch a brow as she eagerly crams food in her mouth.

"Esther." She talks with her mouth full. "How long is he staying? Can we keep him?"

I open my mouth to say, "not long," just as Koa says, "I'm here for the long haul." He winks at me again. We need to have a discussion. Pronto.

I take another tentative bite of food as Koa scrapes his plate clean and starts washing dishes. I stare in pure surprise as he cleans the entire kitchen, yammering on to my sister about the air in Colorado that makes it harder to train for sports, and the humidity in southern Florida that makes it harder still. By the time I finish my breakfast, Koa has tossed a towel over his shoulder, leaned back against the stove, and crossed those burly arms over his chest like I'm in *his* space and he's waiting for my drink order.

Is this what I look like to my customers? Maybe only to the annoying ones. I touch my hair, which is sticking up all over the place, and remember that I'm not wearing a bra. Koa points at me. "I almost forgot your coffee, Hun." He reaches to the back of the stove for a shiny metal coffee-making device I don't think I own. Koa pours me a small mug of the rich brew and starts adding cream. "There we are. Just about the color of a kiwi bird." He smiles as he slides the drink my way.

I'm overcome by the perfection of this drink, certain I'm ruined forever for any other coffee. "What is this? Oh my god." I can't help the moan that escapes my lips, and I tuck my arms over my chest self-consciously before I remember my sister is 19 years old and can handle my nipples and coffee-induced ecstasy.

"Okay, you're being gross." Eva hops up from her seat. "I gotta go." She gives me a quick side hug on her way out of the room and blows Koa a kiss. "Thanks for breakfast!"

I sip my drink luxuriously. The front door clicks shut, and Koa leans forward against the island, his hands tapping on the counter as he watches me eat. "I borrowed your car to go to the shops this morning."

"That's fine."

"You ready to have a talk? We need to make a plan."

I fork another mouthful of food and look at my now-empty coffee mug. Koa sees me staring at it and grins, pouring me a second serving that, from the smell of things, will be just as perfect as the last.

This time he sits next to me in the stool vacated by Eva.

"Right. So, we've got two weeks before Philadelphia. What's our story?"

I close my eyes as I savor the drink. I can't remember the last time someone made me a drink and not the other way around. "Do we need a story? Lots of married people are separated for work travel...you've been coaching all over, right?"

He nods. "True. A season here, two seasons there. You've obviously been busy with your own business here."

"What did you tell my sister?" I whip my head to face him, remembering that no one here knows I'm married... well, they do now. But prior to yesterday, only the court staff was in on the secret. It never felt like anybody's business, although I have often felt bad about holding this back, especially to the Foof ladies who pour their hearts out and lay it all on the table.

He shakes his head. "You heard what I told her. We go way back. I'm here to settle some paperwork. I'll be staying in the primary bedroom with the homeowner." He winks, and this time, there's no mistaking the heat behind the gesture. I like watching his full lips form the word primary.

"Two weeks..." I'm horny, and it's clouding my judgement. Rather than talk to him about our predicament, I start to calculate how much sex I could wring out of him in that amount of time, knowing it's a terrible idea but certain I'll do it anyway. "And then you go again?"

He scratches his chin, leaning back against his stool. "That, I don't know. I don't really have a plan beyond that."

I squint at my coffee, realizing with gratitude that's the thing that will keep me safe from Koa Stewart. There's no need to worry I'll catch feelings for a man with no ambition, no greater purpose. Our bargain gives him the ability to stay here in the country where he's familiar and the freedom to return to his life here if he ever does decide to leave our borders for travel.

I can spend two weeks banging a nomad in my spare time, finagle a day off to sit through an interview in Philadelphia. This will all be a pleasant diversion.

"What should we do to beef up our image? Do you have an alumni event or something? College friends still in town?"

He waves a hand. "Nah. Those lads all have corporate jobs these days. Proper adults." I don't bother telling him he has the same degree from the same university and could join them on the corporate ladder. He's never been interested in that sort of thing. But...he's never really seemed passionate about anything much other than his immigration status.

I set my empty mug down on the counter and tug on the belt of my robe. "Well," I say. "Should we check on your storage unit?"

9

KOA

"Let's take the bike." I phrase this like a suggestion, but there's no way I'm giving up an opportunity to feel Esther pressed against me as I bend and swerve through the city on the way to check out my stuff. Thankfully, she approves of this idea, reaching for a bright red scarf from a hook near the door.

She's right to assume I should want to see my old college mates while I'm in town. After all, I did live in this city for a decade. However, all it does is remind me that I'm still unmoored. What will it take for me to fit in? Not longevity in a place. Not a shared love for a sport, although I do feel more comfortable on the pitch than I do off of it. I wish I knew what I wanted, wish I could explain what drives me to stay in this country.

I do know that this woman right here holds my future in her capable hands. Seeing the home she's created and meeting her sister only served to solidify what I guessed five years ago: Esther is solid. Esther is all that's dependable, and she is rooted to this place. She moves through her realm like she owns it. I smile a bit, knowing I helped her to actually own some of it.

I watch as she ties her hair in a ponytail and folds the scarf around her head. She looks like some glamorous Hollywood actress, especially when she sticks a huge pair of sunnies on her face to complete the look.

I used Esther's laptop while she showered, making sure I still had the code and all the information to look in on my unit. Now, there's nothing to do but inhale my wife as she settles in behind me, the feel of her warm skin fresh from the bath, the clean soapy smell of her. Nothing compares. I haven't been able to shake her out of my head for years, but I convinced myself I was just exaggerating the truth of her in my mind. It's easy to fantasize about the woman with high standards who spent years confiding in me via email.

Esther Storm, or the idea of her anyway, has become my anchor. This woman I write to, who sends me heartfelt messages full of snark and raw honesty. I've got no family, no home, no place I belong, but I had this image of my buxom beauty, like the prow of a ship just bobbing in a safe harbor. And here I am, and she is even better than my idealized notion.

Thinking of her body breaks the rules we set up. This isn't meant to be an emotional attachment. This is business, for her. It should be for me, too.

I circle the lot at the storage place, not because I can't find parking, but because I don't want to lose the feel of her against my back. Eventually, she starts to fidget, so I park the bike and wait as she climbs off. Esther shakes her head as she stashes the helmet, and I smile because I get to watch her do it.

"Is this how you typically spend a day off?" I type the

code to enter the building while Esther smooths out her jeans.

She purses her lips. "Um, I don't usually take days off. If the bar is closed, I work on the books or take care of projects at my house."

"Projects?"

She shrugs. "Yeah. Like cleaning the kitchen, but you took care of that today, so I've got some free time." She kicks at a pebble on the doorstep, and I smile, glad my habitual tidiness won me this time with her.

The door clicks open, and we walk inside, climb a flight of stairs, and navigate the hall of garage doors. The whole place is creepy, the lights flickering due to massive fans along the ceiling. One of the rugby lads in Colorado told me the fans mask the stench of rotting food and unsavory things tenants sneak into their storage bins. I'm not worried about mine. All that's in there is a bit of stuff from my parents' house and a few bins of rugby gear I've been missing.

Then I remember the urn, and I shiver. But I'm sure it's safe, my parents' ashes tucked inside the kauri ash wood box.

"Ah. There we are." I get the lock combination on my first go and heave up the rolling door, revealing tidy stacks of cardboard boxes, all labeled and promptly forgotten by me the night I met Esther. I make my way to RUGBY BOOTS AND SHIRTS and get to work prying open the lid as Esther peers over my shoulder.

"You've been paying to store old shoes and smelly shirts? She wrinkles her nose when she sees my stained All Blacks jersey.

"I promise these are all clean." I give the shirt a shake. "Even stuffed the boots with bicarbonate of soda." I hold out one giant shoe for her to sniff, but she puffs out a laugh and shakes her head.

"I'm not sniffing your shoe, Koa. But come on. You could have stashed these at my place."

"You didn't have much of a place to speak of when I met you." I settle on a cap, two beanies, and two shirts for training in cold weather and close the bin. I give the stack of mum's books a pat. "Plus I didn't even have your number. How could I trust you with my Jonah Lomu kit?"

"I assume Jonah Lomu is a sports baller?"

"Ah, Hun, you're wounding me. Next order of business, we're going to find a rugby match for you to watch with me."

"Pass." Esther taps her nails along one of the boxes, inspecting the ground beneath it. I've got everything stacked on a rubber lift, so I'm not worried about water oozing along the floor. Not that there is any.

"Come on." I lay on my accent thicker than usual. "You'd love it. Sitting on my lap while I whisper the rules in your ear." Esther's cheeks turn pink, and it occurs to me she might actually be down for something like that. I file this valuable information away for later.

"Is there rugby here? In Pittsburgh?"

I nod. "Yeah. I played for a bit in college, coached the ladies a few times."

"How come you never asked one of them to marry you, then?" She crosses her arms over her chest and leans against the wall.

"Dunno. None of them were ever rude to me like you."

"I wasn't rude. I'm just ... not warm."

"Oh, babe, you're plenty warm." I clap my hands. "Speaking of, let's close up. This'll be enough to get started. We need to start banking more memories." Esther makes a confused face as I pull down the garage door and lock the unit. "You know. Selfies on Mt. Washington. Sharing one of those crap sandwiches with the french fries on it. Proof we're mad for each other."

"I'm not eating one of those sandwiches. The fries are always raw. It's disgusting."

"Ah, but you're game for the selfie?"

I usher her outside, tuck my gear in the saddle bag on the bike, and rev the motor a few times as Esther laughs. I head across one bridge, then another as I wind my way up the hill for a good look at the city. So much happened to me here. Once we get to the overlook, I squeeze into a questionable parking spot and lean against the fence, staring at the boats on the river.

This was the first place my parents took me when we left home, and I was grateful we stopped to see the water first thing. I'd been born by the water, raised on the salt air. I felt like a beached whale being yanked from the island and plunked into a strange place. My skin color, my accent, my habits...all of it set me apart.

Rugby was my tether, the link between my homeland and this country, even if the sport here lurks on the fringes of the culture. My dad made sure I found a team to join in high school...a team of adult ex-pats from the UK and Ireland, but they were happy enough to have me since I hulked up at an early age.

"Hey," Esther wraps her arms around me from behind, resting her cheek on my back. "I'm sorry you lost your parents. I should have been nicer at the storage unit, with their things."

I lift an arm and tuck her against my side, still staring out at the confluence of the three rivers. "You know, I wasn't even thinking about them just now? I was missing moana."

"The kids movie?" Esther wriggles her head to stare up at me in confusion.

I shake my head. "Moana," I repeat. "The sea."

"Hm." She stares at the river with me for a bit. "You know, I've never seen the ocean? In real life, I mean."

I stiffen. "Esther. Wife. You've never seen the ocean?" I clutch at my chest and shake my head. "I have to take you there. We have to go. Right now."

She laughs and pushes off my chest. "I can't just leave, Koa. I have responsibilities here."

10

ESTHER

I can tell my words disappoint him, that he wants me to be the kind of person who just picks up and runs away to the ocean because it sounds fun. The kind of person he is, I guess. I sigh and pat his shoulder. "Come on. Take me on an errand."

"And where's that, exactly?" He pushes off the fence, and we walk toward his motorcycle.

"We gotta go to the Jesus store." I shake my hair out of my face and start wedging the helmet on my head. Koa pauses before reaching for his.

"The what?"

"You'll see. Let's move."

I direct him to a tiny shop on Liberty Ave where down-sized convents and churches sell their iconography to people in need. Koa looks skeptical as we walk inside, passing tiny statues of naked cherubs and many, many versions of the Virgin Mary. "Are you Catholic?" he whispers as he wedges himself behind me, sticking close in the packed aisles.

I shake my head and reach for what I need: a huge cardboard box full of prayer candles in clear glass jars. Koa stares as I count out a few dozen candles. "What are you doing?" He nearly trips over the cord for an illuminated Mary on a half shell.

I smile at the clerk and shove the box toward her. "Hi, Ethyl. Just the candles today." I hand her a twenty as she eyes Koa strangely. I hurry out of the shop with my husband in tow. I exhale once we're outside, trying to find the best way to shove all the candles into the bags on his bike.

"This is the cheapest price I can find for candles." I shrug. "I peel off the saint stickers and put the votives on the tables at Bridges and Bitters."

He stares. I shove candles in the motorcycle bags. "Since you asked, sort of, my mother is Jewish. Not practicing." I pause, considering. "That I know of."

Koa scratches the back of his neck. "I wouldn't have thought this place would be open on a Sunday."

"They have brief hours to catch the re-invigorated after Mass. That's my theory." I break down the box, crumple that in the top of the saddlebag, and climb back on the motorcycle. "Okay, take me home. We can scrape while we talk."

Koa mounts the bike again, and I enjoy another opportunity to wrap myself around his big, thick body. He feels unbelievably firm and warm. I can't get enough.

When we get back to the house, I quickly reconstruct the box and put the candles inside, handing Koa the flimsy bundle while I unlock the front door. I'm glad that Eva doesn't appear to be home. I hope she's off studying somewhere. My condition for my sisters staying with me once they turned 18 was that they each had to take at least one class in *something*. I just assumed that would be at the community college where I took business classes to help me run Bridges and Bitters.

Of course Eila found a loophole and started horticulture classes at a technology center, and each of the younger ones followed suit. I have no idea what made any of them care about horticulture. We never even had plants growing up. Maybe that's why? The point is, they're each going into their adventures with a little bit of training and a stable home. They're not flying blind like I was when I tried opening a bar with just a purse full of cash and a little experience as a bartender.

I shoo Koa to the couch and grab the rubbing alcohol from under the kitchen sink. I plunk myself next to him and hand him a paper towel, demonstrating how I use a butterknife to peel off most of the sticker. Soon, we get a rhythm going with me peeling, him dabbing at the residue, and me doing a final wipe and polish.

It's easy to be with him, I realize. Not just physically, but emotionally. We haven't spent much time together, but we just seem to understand each other. Almost like family...but there's nothing familial in how I think of Koa. I'm not sure what to make of my Koa thoughts.

After a few minutes, I nudge him with my shoulder. "So, you still think this was a good idea?"

"What? Buying religious candles for cheap?"

"No!" I laugh at his easy retort. "You know...being stuck with me all this time."

Koa sets the candle and alcohol down on the coffee table and turns to face me. "Marrying you was no hardship, if that's what you're worried about, Esther."

I feel my cheeks heat at the unexpected sincerity in his words. He's been catching me off guard, saying kind things. My voice is quieter than I intend when I clarify, "I just meant, you know, you're sort of stuck here. In the U.S..."

He shrugs. "Here I thought I was doing this because I wanted very badly to stay."

Now it's my turn to set down my work and face him. "I don't get why, though. There's nothing keeping you here. You don't have a real job. I don't think...you don't have any obligations..."

I drift off because I can tell my words are upsetting him. He frowns. "You know I can barely remember anywhere else? I came here when I was just a kid, Esther. And you're right that I have no family. Not here, not in New Zealand. I've got nobody."

I chew on my lip, hating myself for hurting him. I start to apologize, but he continues. "I pay taxes on my inheritance, if you're worried about me being a freeloader or something."

I wince. "Shit. I'm fucking this up. I think...I think maybe I'm jealous? Here you are with fuck-you levels of money, memories of seeing multiple oceans, and with nothing tying you to anywhere. I'd be gone in a heartbeat if I could."

He crosses his arms over his chest and arches a brow. "Would you?" I don't respond, and he leans closer. "You could close the bar for a week. Come with me to the beach. Live it up before we visit immigration." I open my mouth to list all the reasons he's dead wrong about that, but he places a finger over my lips. "I know what you're going to say." He takes a deep breath and picks up the candle again. "Tell me about your sisters."

I realize he only knows surface-level things about them. It wouldn't have made sense for me to explain their history to my husband via email...I've had to be careful what I say to him for so many years, and I really did start to use our messages as opportunities to talk about *me* and my frustrations.

I watch as he continues working, rubbing shiny gold

residue from the bottom of a candle to save me a few bucks. I swallow and start the story I always share. "After my dad ditched me and my mom, she was desperate to find someone again. To feel needed. But it was the same thing again and again...a baby, the reality of that, and then he'd be gone. I'm not actually sure who Eila and Eliza's fathers are... but the four girls showed up fast and got in the way of Mom finding that elusive true love."

Koa nods. "And someone had to look after them, right? Get them off to school and do their laundry and scrape together a grocery order?"

I nod as he keeps working. "Someone did."

I look out the front window to see Eva approaching with an armful of papers and plants. Koa smiles. "Looks like you finished the job, then." He seems so smug, like I can turn off the years of parenting my sisters just because they arbitrarily hit some threshold where the government defines them as adults. The age he was when he lost his parents, I realize.

Eva makes her way in the door and hustles upstairs with a shout about studying or something along those lines. I remember once more that I did this for my sisters. I married this guy to get that wad of cash to make a better life for the five of us. I don't need a partner—not Koa and not anyone else. Someday, the Storm sisters will go and see the ocean together. I don't need anyone, especially this man, judging me for taking care of my family. He's leaving. Just like everyone else in our lives has always done.

11

KOA

After we repurpose the holy candles, Esther retreats to her room, and I use her laptop again to check my email. I've got all her messages to me in their own inbox where I can reread them at night when I'm feeling low.

I don't need that version of Esther right now, though. I'm right here with her, in her house.

I have been waiting to hear back from a few different teams, however, regarding where I might go next, but this Philadelphia interlude came at a kind of inopportune time.

Everyone's wrapping up their spring season and nobody seems to have a stipend to pay a coach in the summer. I consider telling the New Orleans team I'll help out for free. It'd be cool to spend the summer down south. Or maybe I should find a team near a beach. Learn to surf again...

"Eva, you coming to see the bees?" Esther yells down to her sister, and I close the lid of the laptop, intrigued.

"Be ready in a minute," Eva hollers back.

I poke my head into the dining room where Eva is fixing her hair in the mirror. "Did she say bees?"

Eva nods with a hair pin between her teeth. "Eden has beehives in her backyard, and Esther buys the honey for cocktails. I think."

"Does she wear a proper bee suit and all that?" Eva nods. "This I have to see." She shrugs and walks out the front door. I follow and wait with her by Esther's car, meeting my wife's gaze as she heads toward us, a giant jar in each hand.

"You're coming with us?"

"Haven't I been helping you all day? Can't rightly miss this adventure, can I?"

Esther hesitates but unlocks the car. I haven't met the other Storm sisters yet, and Esther hasn't agreed to talk through what we'll tell them, so I take matters into my own hands. "Eva." I turn in my seat to face her, and she looks up from her phone, her teenaged expression conveying a whole bunch of *yeah???* "What do your sisters know about me?"

She flinches. "Um, nothing? I barely know about you."

Esther groans and pulls into a parking space by a vacant lot. Upon closer inspection, it's not fully vacant. I see brightly colored bee boxes and some deliberate plants climbing a trellis.

Two dark-haired women emerge from the house next-door, and I can tell immediately they're Esther's sisters. They swoop in on the car, one of them grabbing the jars and the other thrusting work gloves into Eva's hands. Neither of them registers my presence, and I step aside as one—assuming that's Eden—puffs smoke into a bee box from a rusty canister.

I look to Eva, who is taking her time pulling on the gloves. "I thought you said she wears a bee suit?"

Eva looks up at her sister and shrugs. "The bees must not be angry today. She says she can sense their mood or whatever."

A few minutes later, Eden approaches with a five-gallon bucket full of dripping honeycomb. I barely noticed her doing anything back at the hive. Esther and Eila are bent over, sniffing plants, and I force myself to look away from Esther's backside as Eva and Eden struggle with the bucket.

"Here," I reach out a hand. "I got it."

Eden pauses. "Who the hell are you?"

Eva hooks a gloved thumb at me. "This is Koa. He's staying with Esther. I don't think they're banging."

"Gross, Eva." Eden wrinkles her nose. "Staying with Esther how? Like at the chalet?"

Eva nods. "He cooks breakfast and makes Esther let him help her."

This brings a smile to Eden's face, and she pulls out a phone. I watch, holding the heavy bucket, as she sends a text message. Nodding, Eden points toward a metal contraption behind the house. "Come on, Koa. We're going to spin the honey."

I follow her instructions, set the comb up in the centrifuge, and watch as she slowly cranks the handle. Soon enough, she gestures toward Eva, who hands her the giant jar.

"Say, what's Esther doing over there with Eila, anyway?"

Eden doesn't look up from the spout as she pours the nectar. "Eila is trying to convince Esther to order some beer. Those are hops plants she's growing." She caps the jar and beams at me. "My bees love them." I nod, and Eden hands me the full jar. It's warm, and I hold it up to the sun, admiring. She smirks at me. "You're helping Esther?"

I lower the jar and meet her gaze. "We're helping each other out, she and I. We have a bargain."

Eva shakes her head. "Nah. It's more than that. He made her coffee and served her food."

A truck pulls up at the curb, and I watch as another Storm sister climbs out. It must be Eliza. She strides toward us in the yard, hands in the pockets of her overalls. "You said there's a meeting?"

Esther pokes her head up from the hops trellis and frowns at Eliza. "I thought you were doing flea treatments all day?"

Hands on her hips, Eliza lifts her brows. "Eden said we're having a meeting."

The five Storm girls converge around me as Eden hands me a second jar of honey. It's gorgeous, a dark amber color. I marvel that a minute ago, it was inside a beehive twenty meters away from me. Something so sweet came from such a precarious environment.

Eden points at me as I hold the honey. "Esther has some news," Eden says. "I figure it's better if we all hear it at once."

Eva procures a bag of chips from her purse and passes them around to her sisters. They all sink to sit on up-turned buckets and logs that pepper the yard while Esther remains standing, eyes toward the heavens. "Look," she tells them. "You know I found an investor all those years ago to open the bar and buy the house."

"Ooh, is Koa your adventure capitalist?" Eva munches a handful of chips. I don't correct her terminology, but I grin, waiting to learn what story Esther told the girls to explain the sudden appearance of money and stability in their lives.

"It wasn't so much an investment as it was a bargain. An even trade." Esther kicks at some debris with her boot.

Eila presses her lips together. "An even trade?" She looks to me. "Koa, what did Esther trade you that was even for a bazillion dollars?"

Esther's chest rises and falls rapidly, and she looks sweaty. This might be the first time either of us has explained this to anyone else. "It's just a paperwork thing." I repeat the half-truth I gave Eva earlier this morning, holding my thumb and forefinger close together. "Esther gave me a little help with my immigration status."

Eliza bleats out a laugh, sounding exactly like the goats I hear she tends for a living. "Don't tell me," she laughs. "You're doing a marriage of convenience? Like from one of Chloe's books?"

Her laughter slowly fades as nobody else joins her. Eila's mouth hangs open, and Eden starts munching on raw honeycomb. I had no idea it was edible. Esther finally sits, her face in her hands as she shakes her head. "Wait," Eliza points at me. "That's really it? You guys got married, and you gave her a bunch of money?"

I'm about to explain...I'm not even sure what, but I don't get a chance, because Esther's four sisters maul me in an eight-armed tackle-hug. They squeeze me until I feel like I'm being reborn, each of them talking over top of the other as they shout, "You bought us a home?" "You took care of us?" and the like.

Esther looks up and meets my eye where my head sticks up from the scrum of Storms. I hadn't considered the impact our bargain would have on Esther's sisters. I knew she cared for them when she agreed to do this, but I never stopped to think that giving Esther money meant investing in them, too.

Eventually, they all let go and move to hug their eldest sister. "Why don't you ever tell us anything?" Eden wags a finger at Esther. "We can handle shit, you know? We learned it from you."

12

ESTHER

I wake again to the smell of breakfast cooking. *I could get used to this...*

The instant I think it, I scold myself for doing so. I shouldn't get used to any of it. Appreciate it for what it is: fleeting, a nice treat while Koa is in town.

When I make my way to the kitchen, he's plating an omelet on the counter beside a steaming mug of coffee. I forget that I'm irritated with him, and I dig into the food before I remember to greet him.

"That good, eh?" He laughs at me as he walks around the island with his own plate, heaving himself into a stool beside me at the counter.

I swallow the food. "You know it's good. It could taste like anything, and I'd love it because I didn't make it. But you know it's good."

He winks. Always with the winking. I wonder if his eye muscles get tired. Then I sip my coffee until I don't care about winking or eye muscles. So good.

"Eva left for class but wanted me to tell you she ran the laundry this morning."

I smirk at him. My sisters aren't helpless, but I can tell he thinks they are. Or that I baby them. Or something.

"She says you're out of detergent." My heart sinks a tiny bit at that because I don't charge my sisters rent, and I certainly don't invoice them for food or shampoo.

I sigh. "Hopefully she'll grab some when she's out today."

"You think so?" Koa chews smugly. He's sending smug vibes this morning. I growl at him, inwardly. Then he sets his fork down. "I think we should pop into a clinic for some physicals before we head to Philadelphia."

I scowl at him. "Why? I feel fine."

He scowls at me. "We want to head off anything that might send the wrong message."

"You think they'll check our blood?"

"You think they won't?" Koa crosses his arms over his substantial chest and shakes his head. "Esther, they're going to test me for everything under the sun. TB, bird flu, mad cow..."

"What about me?"

He shrugs. "All I'm saying is an ounce of prevention..."

I drink more coffee. He stares at me. "Were you going to finish that sentence?" He arches a brow and I sigh. "Fine. We can go to a clinic this morning. I know a guy who does walk-ins."

"You know a guy? Is this clinic really a van in an alley?"

I give him a playful smack. "It's a legit doctor in East Liberty. We can go to Target after."

"Oooh, Target. My favorite," he teases before kissing me on the cheek. I have to convince myself not to get used to that, either.

AN HOUR LATER, we wait our turn for a blood draw at the iHealth clinic. Koa barely fits in the chairs in the waiting room, and I stare at his frame, trying not to drool. He catches me looking and smiles. "Tell me more about your life, Wife. Who were all those women at the bar asking about me?"

I smile without thinking. "Foof," I say. "Fresh out of fucks. You met Sam, Piper, and Chloe, but there are a bunch of us. We meet at the bar a few times a month."

"Meet for what?"

I hum out a laugh. "To smash the patriarchy." My smile widens as I remember when I first opened the bar, Samantha stumbled in looking for someone to tell about the amazing company she just formed from her dorm room. I pat Koa's arm. "We mostly support each other. Give pep talks if someone's applying for a job, or quitting a job, or running for office."

His face twitches. "You know elected officials? You might have mentioned that, Esther."

I wave a hand. "Juniper Jones is a judge in family court. She's too busy protecting children to worry about a sham marriage." He stiffens uncomfortably at my words. I hasten to add, "not that this is a sham. We are one hundred per cent in love, preparing for a healthy honeymoon."

Koa's eyes fly wide, and I wince. "I'm sorry," I whisper. "I usually don't talk about this at all. There's nobody here, though..."

Again, I remember that I've been keeping this secret even from Foof, that I haven't been honest with them in the ways they've been brave and vulnerable with me. I never wanted to admit to them that I built my cocktail empire, as Sam calls it, on a nefarious bargain. I like that they think I built it brick by brick, like a badass, as they all did with their own careers.

My sisters never ask questions. They're used to me doing whatever needs to be done, and I prefer it when they aren't aware of any sacrifices I've made to make sure they're okay. But Foof? I'm going to have to face them, and soon.

"Mr. and Mrs. Stewart?" A nurse pops his head through the door, looking around the empty waiting room as if we couldn't possibly be the couple in question.

"Mr. Stewart and Ms. Storm, if you please." Koa rises to his feet and offers me a hand. He always surprises me with these small things, like he knew I'd never change my name, or that changed names have nothing to do with the truth of a marriage.

"My apologies. If you both follow me, we can get started on the testing."

There's barely room for the two of us in the tiny exam room. The nurse swabs our nostrils and our throats, pricks our fingers, and asks us who will go first for the blood draw. Koa is silent, which is very unlike him. When I glance toward him, he looks clammy. "Don't tell me you're afraid of needles?"

He shakes his head but doesn't answer.

"Koa. You have a tattoo. You're Māori. You're really—"

"I'd prefer if you went first." He snaps the words and closes his eyes. I watch his powerful throat swallow and shake my head before telling the nurse to just strap the tourniquet around my arm.

While the nurse—his name tag says Chao—works on my left arm, I turn in the chair toward Koa, rubbing his leg. "Hey. What's up?"

He keeps his eyes closed but places his hand on mine. "I do not like needles. It's the piercing...it gives me the shivers."

I press my lips together at his adorable turn of phrase. "I'll hold your hand. It'll be okay."

"I know it will. I'll be ready when it's my turn."

"You should get some water, Koa. Go in the hall—I saw a fountain."

He shakes his head. "If I leave this chair, I won't sit back in it. Better in and out and then I'll hydrate." Chao looks at me, concerned, and looks at Koa.

With a flick and a quick piece of tape, I'm set free from the blood draw, and I spin 90 degrees toward my giant Pacific Islander. "Babe. Squeeze my hand. Do you want to look in my eyes or keep them closed?"

"Closed," he bursts out as Chao slides around the chair and dabs an alcohol rub on Koa's forearm.

"Little pinch," he says, and Koa stiffens.

"Hey, wiggle your fingers," I soothe, and he does. Chao looks relieved, and I peek around Koa's bulk to see he's almost filled the vial already. "Almost done."

Koa sags in relief when the nurse pulls the needle from his arm and tells us we can take our time. The lab will call with results in a few days. Alone in the room, I take Koa's face in my hands. "Have you always been scared of needles?"

He nods his head. "My parents had very little tolerance for it. We needed a lot of tests to come to this country initially..."

"That must have been scary." I press a kiss to his forehead, surprising both of us. I don't typically experience feelings of tenderness. Who has time? I can hear his heart pounding in his chest as I hug him, and I hurry to climb to my feet. "Okay, well, we need to head into Target. Apparently, I need laundry detergent."

With a groan and a scoff, Koa follows me down the hall.

13

KOA

We have just about a week before our interview in Philadelphia, and I can't get Esther to discuss it. We had a clean bill of health, and her sisters are on board. We've been having photo shoots and making omelets, and I treasure all our time together... but I'm getting anxious.

Esther told me I mustn't come to her bar tonight because she plans to tell her friends a bit about our situation. I see no reason to heed this request, especially since she said some of them are lawyers, so I hover around the door and watch as she disappears down the hall with a tray of drinks before I slide inside.

I see Ruthie behind the bar and give her a nod as I position myself on a stool at the far end of the bar.

I can hear the shrieks and commotion from here.

"You going to go listen at the door?" Ruthie raises an eyebrow at me as she slides me a bottle of beer. I consider her question and she continues. "Because if you're not, then can you watch the bar while I go listen?"

"Ha! Let's not put me in charge of mixing drinks.

Although, it seems like most of the takers are back there squealing at Esther."

Ruthie gestures for me to go down the hall, and I tip my beer at her before slinking into the shadow to find out what I can overhear.

A blonde woman gestures wildly, pacing as she taps away at her phone. "I'm texting AJ right now. He can't handle another day of me speculating. Esther, we've been freaking out since the book launch."

"You can't bring a man to a Foof meeting, Sam," Esther insists.

Another woman—the one I caught rooting in the closet—asks why. "Men can help smash the patriarchy, Esther. We need men to do that, I think."

"Agreed!" A largely pregnant woman with wildly curly hair pounds her fist on the table, and I forget that I'm trying to be sneaky, letting out a laugh.

"What was that?" I bite my lip, but a group of women approach the door and peek into the hall. "Aha! He's here!"

I'm hauled into the room before I can think twice, and if I'm honest, I'm glad to be meeting Esther's friends. I want to be shown off as her husband. Which makes no sense at all because even I thought the agreement was that we handle this paperwork and each move on with our lives.

"Hello," I say, a bit awkwardly. Esther looks like a tomato, and I'm a bit worried she will grab the chrome pipe she uses to intimidate inappropriate patrons.

"Sit," says the blonde woman, pointing beside her on a velvet fainting couch. "Spill your guts."

"Don't mind if I do." I make my way over, consider kissing Esther on the cheek, but then change course when I feel that her aura is sending dangerous signals. "I'm Koa, the husband. I'm taking Esther on a wee bit of a holiday."

She's been in denial long enough, and I'm not ashamed of my tactics here with her friends. Esther looks like a volcano about to erupt.

The women lean forward, chins on hands, elbows on the table, rapt. I clear my throat. "I hear you all are fresh out of fucks. I don't blame you a bit. I'm fresh out of a lot of things."

Esther rolls her eyes. "He's here for another week. We have a meeting in Philadelphia. This is not a big deal."

The blonde shakes her head. "This is a big deal. I'm Samantha Vine, by the way. My friend Esther has been very rude. Do you want me to introduce you to everyone? I guess there's a lot of us...if you needed legal help you should have gone to Judge Juniper."

Someone else nods and pats my arm. "If you need money help you should call Logan Brady."

"Cheers, gals. I'm all set with my finances, and I'm not in trouble. Like Esther said, we just have a meeting is all. Where should I take her for dinner in Philly?"

This changes the tone and soon enough a silver-haired grandma is telling us all about a very strange Philadelphia museum full of body parts, conveniently located a few blocks from a fantastic restaurant.

Esther purses her lips and grabs a glass of alcohol. She swigs a big gulp and says, "Thank you, Celeste. That sounds like a great outing."

Celeste smiles and pats Esther's hand. "Don't skip the collection of things children swallowed. I took my grandchildren there as a precautionary tale."

Before anyone can comment further, a trio of men appear at the door. I recognize them from the book party I crashed and give a wave. My biggest takeaway from all this chaos is that Esther is surrounded by invested people.

Grandmas and lawyers and financiers. Pals and sisters. She's got everything. And I've got her. Temporarily at least.

The meeting is clearly disrupted, and people start leaving the back room. Esther remains seated at the table chugging cocktails.

"Easy there, pet." I take a look at the expression on her face and grin. "Just a test. I know you're not my pet." I pat her hand. "You're my treasure."

I receive an eye roll for that line, but I'll take it since she follows it up by sagging her beautiful body against my side. "None of them asked me how I feel about all this."

I risk running a hand through her hair, and she seems soothed by this motion, so I continue. "How do you feel about all this?"

She shrugs. "I don't fucking know. I've avoided thinking about it since you left me that big, fat cashier's check."

"And now, here I am."

"Here you are." She leans back enough to look me in the eye. "You're turning my life inside-out."

"Esther, all I did was ask you to come to Philadelphia for a meeting."

She shakes her head. "No. You mailed me candy and crystals. You cleaned my kitchen and made my sister eggs, and I'm pretty sure you dusted all the ceiling fans."

I nod. "I did do that. It seemed necessary."

Esther blows a raspberry. "I should have remembered to do that. I could have taped the feather duster to a yard stick or something."

"A meterstick would get you a bit more length..."

She smacks my arm. "Why won't you admit that you're ruining everything?"

"And just how am I doing that?"

"You've made me drink while I'm at work, and I never do

that. And you're just walking around all sexy and huge and it makes me want to break all my rules."

I feel a lick of flame along my spine at her confession that she finds me sexy, still. "We're breaking a fair number of rules together. What's one more?"

She shakes her head. "I can't do that, even though it would be great. I'm tapped out for emotional investment, Koa. Tapped like a keg of weird beer my sister made and my clients seem to like even if I wish they wouldn't."

"How about I take you home and you can recharge with some sleep, eh?"

She flops her head onto her hands, hair tumbling across her face. "I'm mean and making you sleep on the sofa bed."

"I don't mind," I lie. "I like being in the room with you." That part's the truth. "You're like a fern, stubborn and strong."

"I know." Esther smiles dreamily.

I stroke her hair. "Ferns are really special to me, you know." I want to tell her everything, share all the stories my family has always told about the silvery ponga trees that only grow in New Zealand.

She shakes her head again. "I can't do it, Koa. I can't let myself fall for you. I won't risk it."

I stiffen a bit and stand, offering her my hand. "Let's get you some water and a bed, Hun. We can talk later."

I drive home as she mutters on repeat, insisting again and again that there's absolutely no way she can make room for me in her black, shriveled heart.

I know it's true, and I feel the same. But that doesn't explain why it stings to hear her say it, why it feels so empty to lie near her but not touch. Why the foot between her bed and mine feels as broad as the chasm between our two lives.

14

ESTHER

I don't have time to be hungover, yet here I am. I groan, cursing the strong drinks I made my friends and the urge to chug them after Koa invaded our Foof meeting.

But then I roll over and see a glass of water by my bedside and three aspirin on a little dish. I stare at the dish. I do not think I own little white dishes the perfect size for a dose of aspirin. I know Koa did all this, and I remember all the emotions I leaked last night. I remember Samantha screaming that I finally confessed to being a human being with human weaknesses and everyone else smiling in relief.

I remember telling Koa how he makes me want to break the rules. I hesitate, staring at the altar of caregiving next to me.

Eventually I take the offerings and work my way downstairs, filling my arms with laundry from the bathrooms along the way. As I shove the towels into the washer, I see Koa frowning over my laptop.

He's dressed neatly, clearly showered, with his bare, brown toes curled around the rung of the stool. It's the toes that really get me. He obviously feels comfortable here, but he's not being a mooch. He found me a magic aspirin dish, for fuck's sake.

"Hey," I say, and then he turns to face me, smiling, and it takes my breath away. I had no idea it was possible to feel this attracted to another person. I feel a momentary sense of understanding for my mother—the way she lets herself get swept up in men. Is this how she feels each time? I need to be careful.

"Morning, gorgeous. How's your head?"

"Better, thank you." I curl my lips in and tap the counter. "Where did you get that little dish thing? For the aspirin?"

"It's a salt dish. Found it in your spice cupboard. And I hope you don't mind, but I threw out a lot of those. They were dated before you and I met. Did you move them here from your rat hole?"

I wander around the counter in search of coffee and can't hold back the squeal when I see he's made me another mug of his magic brew. I take a big sip. "I pretty much just tossed everything into a box and yes, put it away. My sisters brought some stuff..."

"Like oregano that expired six years ago." He grins. "What's on the agenda today? Dumpster diving for bar nuts?"

I groan and shake my head at him. "I don't know why I use the Jesus candles. It's not like I cut corners anywhere else at the bar. I think it's an old habit I can't quit."

I feel his hand on my back. It's warm and huge and comforting. "I'll stop teasing you about it someday."

I drink my coffee in silence until my phone rings. I glance down and see that it's Piper calling. "Hey," I say, watching as Koa returns to his web browser.

"Esther, I know it's last minute, but can you do a lunch thing at the gym today?"

"Lunch at the gym?" I know how Piper eats. I'm not interested in a lumpy green shake full of whey protein.

"It's a whole thing for donors. Remember how you wouldn't let me give you back the money, so I donated it to the women's wellness center?"

I nod, remember that she can't see me, and tell her, "It sounds familiar."

"Right, well they decided to name the snack bar after you! Esther's Eats."

"Oh, god, is that name final?"

"I'm sure you can workshop it. But today's the opening..."

I sigh and run a hand through my hair. I look at Koa. "Can I bring my husband?"

"Ha! See you in two hours."

KOA INSISTS on driving us on his motorcycle which means I spend an entire twenty minutes pressed against his hot body. I mean literally hot—he radiates just enough warmth that I'm not cold as he zooms along Route 28 toward the Highland Park bridge. I forget that he grew up here, or at least spent ten years living in Pittsburgh before he skipped town to be a nomad.

We both acknowledged that a photo op at this event would be good for his immigration file. I didn't explain that I'd given a bunch of money to Piper last year when she was opening her own business. Bridges and Bitters was profitable from the get-go, and I had money to burn. I could have saved it for my sisters, I guess. But it felt good to support Piper, and I really like what she's doing, supporting moms. Maybe if my mom felt supported by other women, she wouldn't have been so desperate for a man to love her. I don't know.

"This place seems nice," Koa says, reaching for my helmet and stashing both inside the seat of his motorcycle.

"It's pretty cool. There's a childcare."

He smiles. "I can see why you invested in a random cafe across town. If there's childcare…"

"Very funny."

We walk inside to find Cash sitting on the floor and playing a guitar, surrounded by clapping children. Piper's humongous boyfriend is usually gruffer than me, so it's hilarious to see him singing silly songs with kids. I guess he is a dad, and he's dating Piper, so she's probably rubbing off on him.

I glance at Koa, who sinks to the floor by the kids to clap along with the song, and briefly wonder if being with him would put me in a cheerful mood. I shake off that thought and stride over to Piper who is beaming.

"The name is not set in stone," she says by way of greeting. "They just needed something for the chalk board today. You ready for pics?"

"Wow, okay, we're moving right into it." I straighten out my top and run my fingers through my hair.

Piper shrugs. "You're always busy. I wanted to be respectful of your time. Aw, look at Koa hanging out with Cash and the little ones." She swats my arm. "He's cute."

He's more than cute. He's gorgeous. But I'm not going to say so. "Who is taking the photos?"

Piper points to a guy with a camera, currently taking a thousand pictures of Cash and Koa. "I thought the building owner would be here today since he asked me to call you.

But he just sent a photographer. There's a yoga class in session right now, and the cafe is giving away muffins after. Maybe you could hand out some muffins and smile?"

"Wait. You need me to run service?" I look down at my dark jeans and top. I suppose I'm dressed for the part, but I wasn't expecting to work with food today.

Piper shakes her head. "Just one or two for a photo. The muffins are all plated and such. Teniola is in charge of all that." Piper waves at the woman in a Nigerian flag t-shirt. I feel a wash of relief.

"Sure. I can hand out a few muffins for posterity."

"I hope they go right to your posterior." Koa smacks my behind, making me jump. It should feel invasive or too familiar or something...but it just feels right.

"I thought you were singing."

"Didn't want to miss the red carpet." He gestures toward the photographer, who has started shooting candids of Koa and me.

We turn to smile at him properly, and Koa slips an arm around my shoulders like he was born doing it. And the funny thing is that it doesn't feel foreign. It's nice, touching him. Posing for photos with him to celebrate the way I chose to spend his damn money.

No, I remind myself. It's my money, in exchange for lending him my citizenship. And five years of tell-all emails where I inexplicably unloaded my burdens on him. Either way, we both smile and hand out muffins to a group of women who seem grateful to receive them. By the time Koa is dropping me off at my bar, I decide there are worse ways to spend an afternoon.

15

KOA

As per usual, I wake well before anyone else in the Storm household. I leave for a run and wind up miles away, on campus where my parents taught and where I attended uni. And here I sit on a bench, hours later, marveling that this is the place that turned my whole world upside-down.

Most days I try not to think about it, but today I'm pissed off about the lot. How did I end up this way? Drifting around all alone? Esther's right—I could be building some sort of stability. I have a degree. I have a fuck-ton of money I don't know how to spend. How is it that nothing fits? Nothing feels right...except Esther. And she's off limits.

Sitting in a puddle of my own sweat, I dread the long slog home...well, that's not the right word, is it? I don't have a home. Esther was crystal clear about that. I don't belong here, in this country, in her house, and definitely not in her bed.

What pisses me off the most about all of it is that she's right. I have no clue where I'm going or why, and this list-lessness drives me mad when I let it.

I'm not a New Zealander or an American. If I did leave this place, I'd be just as much an outsider in Aotearoa as I am here. At least here I have an edge when it comes to coaching...

I'm about to saunter off campus into a pub and drink myself calm when I see someone I know. One of Esther's friends is leading a group of women through an exercise class over on the football pitch.

I walk a bit closer to make sure I'm not seeing things, but it's her. Piper, from the muffin building, cheering on her class as they work through a long plank hold. I take a bit of a lean on the fence to see what's up and soon, Piper ends the class with hugs and high fives all around. I wait until most of the students have gone before I walk up to her with a "hey" so as not to startle her.

Piper whips her head around, and her mouth forms an "oh" as she recognizes me. "Ooh, Esther's husband. Fancy meeting you here."

"I could say the same. Minus the husband bit."

She waves a hand. "It's a nice day, and I wanted to hold class outdoors for a change." She pauses. "You look like you use the gym. A lot. I know I said that before."

I tip my hand in a so-so gesture. "I keep fit." There's an awkward silence where she seems like she wants me to spill my guts but doesn't want to pry. "Tell you what, Piper. Give me a ride, and I'll tell you anything you want to know."

"Oh, I love this plan. Let me just tell Cash I'll be late. Or would he want to come and hear the tea? No. He's not into gossip." She rambles to herself, tapping away at her phone. "Okay, so for starters, how on earth are you married to Esther? I gotta here how you wooed her, man."

"It's a paperwork thing." I follow her as she walks up the

grassy hill to a bright green car that I don't know I can fit inside. "You can maybe tell I wasn't born here."

She snorts. "The accent is definitely either Aussie or Kiwi. New Zealand is on my bucket list of places to visit someday. Can you imagine Cash exploring hobbit holes with me?"

"I take it he's not a Tolkien fan?"

She smiles. "He's got the beard for it." I wedge myself in the car and manage to buckle my seatbelt before she pulls onto the road. "I think he enjoys reading the books to our daughter, but he's not the type of guy to squeal about a movie set." Piper offers me a bottle of water from her console, and I take it gratefully. "Did you run here all the way from Esther's place?" I nod and wipe my mouth with the back of my hand. "Did you...did you know she invested in my business?"

My brows shoot up. "I did not, no. That was good of her." I can tell Esther does all right for herself by the look of her home and the state of her bar.

Piper nods. "Yeah, that's what yesterday was about. She refused to let me pay her back, so her donation went to the women's wellness center. They named the cafe after her."

"I saw that much." I scratch my chin. "Interesting." If Esther has enough money to throw away and not care about it, then she has absolutely no motivation to stay tangled in a paperwork marriage. Esther has always done exactly as she says she would. "Well, we struck a deal, she and I. She got the funds to buy Bridges and Bitters, and I get to stick around the U.S. indefinitely."

"Hmm. I didn't know it was that easy to get citizenship."

"Oh, I'm nowhere close to that. Right now, I'm just...an American's husband in limbo." I turn a bit to face her better. "I'm trying to get Esther to come on holiday with me, live it up a bit before we have an immigration meeting in Philadelphia."

Piper snorts again. "Good luck with that! Sam sometimes gets her to get pedicures with the gals, but even that's like pulling teeth. Do you know Esther works every day?"

"I'm aware. Sunday was candle peeling."

"Oh! I've helped with that before. Every now and then we get a scented one in the box, but it's never what you'd call a pleasing smell."

"Probably like me right now." I tug at my shirt as Piper pulls up in front of Esther's house. "I appreciate the lift, Piper. You coming inside?"

"Well, since I'm here anyway..." She cackles and hops out of the car, practically skipping up the steps to the front door. When we get inside, Esther is pouting on the couch, arms crossed, surrounded by all four of her sisters.

Piper claps her hands. "Oh, nice. The Storms are all here. This is going to be good. I brought Koa home for you." Piper winks and perches herself on the arm of the sofa. Esther looks murderous. It's adorable.

16

ESTHER

I'm not sure how my life became so complicated all of a sudden. I was just fine, business was booming, and I was leaning into my friendships, getting some no-strings nooky when I felt like it. Now it seems like my entire world has exploded.

My estranged husband showed up out of nowhere to try to get me to take a beach vacation, and my sister failed out of her horticulture program. Worse, all my other sisters showed up one after the other with their own annoying problems like IRS letters and abnormal PAP results. Now, I'm just surrounded by angst and big feelings.

I tried interrupting their drama to explain the bare bones of my business arrangement, maybe let them know they might start hearing from immigration folks. But that revelation just triggered more wails and woes on their part.

By the time Piper bursts into my house with Koa in tow, I feel like a tea kettle ready to whistle.

It doesn't help that Eva drapes herself over Koa, weeping onto his shoulder like she's known him for decades. To my surprise, he pulls her close and rubs her back, humming sympathetically as she wails about unfair policies.

"Right." Piper claps her hands and wriggles onto the couch next to Eila. She puts on a face I'm not familiar with and enters instructor mode. I cross my arms and lean back. Piper points at Eva. "Honey, we've all failed things. Remember last year when my entire business got shut down? I got through that. You'll get through this."

Eva sniffs and extracts herself from our house guest. "Yeah, but you weren't *homeless* at least. I'm going to have to live in a trailer or something with my *mother.*"

My eyebrows shoot up. "Is that what you think? That I'd kick you out?"

She sniffles. "You said it was a firm rule." She puts on a mock stern voice. "If you wanna stay under this roof, you're going to get some education."

Apparently, a lot of my firm rules are actually bendable. I try not to look at Koa as I lean forward and squeeze her leg. "Honey, I'm not kicking you out on the street. Besides, even if I did, you could go stay with Eila and Eden."

The Storm sisters in question huff and mutter something about no space. I shoot them a death glare, and Eva nods. "I just feel like such a burden. The rest of you do all this great stuff."

I throw my hands up. "Oh, yeah, so great. Eila's getting audited, and Eden has gonorrhea. I have to go visit immigration with my paperwork-husband, and I can't even manage to hire a bar manager. Face it, Eva. We've all got hurdles."

Eden leans across Eliza and jabs a finger into my bicep, hard. "Ouch!"

"Gonorrhea is very common," my sister growls. "It's fully treatable."

"Then why the hell are you here on my couch sobbing

about it?" I rub my arm, irritated.

Koa seems thoroughly amused by the entire proceeding, not horrified, even at the mention of a sexually transmitted infection. "Can I make a suggestion?" He approaches the question with hesitation, as if he can tell everyone is on the verge of pulling hair.

I gesture for him to continue.

He scratches his chin. "Right. So, Eden, have you called your doctor?"

She blinks at him and shrugs. He points an index finger at her. "These things happen all the time, honest. Have you started the meds?" When Eden nods, Koa turns to face Eila.

"Next. Eila. Have you touched based with your sister's money wizard friend? Pipes, what's her name?"

"Logan." Piper grins and leans forward, elbows on her knees.

"Eila, why don't you get Logan's information from Piper and sort out your money issues. Eliza, you're just here for the show, aren't you?"

She shrugs. "I drove."

Koa waves a hand at her. "Eva needs to sort out her life, and Esther needs to take time off for some very important business related to yours truly." He points at himself and winks. I think my sisters swoon. "What if—now, Esther, I want you to hear the whole thing before you growl and pack a sad. What if Eva minds the bar for a bit while you and I take care of things?"

My snap response is obviously to insist this is a terrible idea, but Piper steamrolls the entire conversation. "Oh, excellent. Koa, I like this plan. Eva's worked the bar a bunch anyway and knows how to make all your drinks. And this is sort of a slow time of year when all the college students are gone but hot girl summer hasn't quite started yet."

Eliza taps her nails on her arm. "It's my busy season, so I can't be backup."

Eva stands up. "I love this idea. I can do this. I can manage Bridges for a week. No sweat. I mean, some sweat, obviously, because it'll be busy. But you'll show me what to order and when and it'll be easy peasy."

Eila furrows her brow. "I can't really think of any downsides to this other than Esther having to relinquish control for a hot minute."

"It'll take her four days just to unclench," Eden adds, and then ducks when I move to tug on her ponytail.

"I can't just up and leave. That's not how it works as a business owner."

Koa scowls, incredulous. "You're telling me not a single business owner has ever gone on holiday?"

I roll my eyes at him. "Maybe where you come from. Don't you know that Americans don't know how to take it easy?" I wince, then, because I heard myself othering him, remembering he's sensitive to his nomad status.

"Yeah, Esther, I do know that. And look where that attitude got my parents. Worked their asses off until they forgot my paperwork wasn't sorted and then died in a wreck without ever taking a deep breath. Is that how you want your life to go?"

His nostrils flare as he delivers this speech, and I can feel the tension radiating from his body. I want to wrap my arms around him, to comfort the boy who was Eva's age and left to face the world alone. He didn't have a sister to step in when his parents weren't there. I realize I have tears welling in my eyes.

There's a long silence while everyone ingests his words. Koa has always been the afterthought from the "more important" work his parents had going on, and I'm in a position to change that. But I'm resisting leaving town for a few days to do what needs to be done. For what? Where does this hesitation come from?

Because I don't know how to let go, even a little, is what I won't say out loud. Because each time I tried to let go a little, one of my sisters got strep or called me at prom because someone threw up. I stare around the room, at each of them in turn, wondering what the young-adult version of these disasters might be if I tried going to the beach.

Finally, Piper jumps up from her seat and wraps her arms around my big, burly husband. "Koa, I'm so sorry. I lost my mom real young, too. Parent loss is just beyond."

And there it is. The reminder that I have no capacity to care for anyone additional. I keep forgetting that Koa is grieving. That he's suffered a massive loss. I should comfort him, like Piper is.

He hugs her back and then extracts himself like he wasn't planning on handling his own emotions, but only meting out instructions for my sisters. "Cheers, bruv."

Everyone turns to me, silently, waiting to hear what's going to happen next. I look at each of them, at the sisters who are having challenges, but don't require emergent rescue. At the trio of dark-haired, capable women offering to run backup for Eva, who is young but determined, despite her struggle to get up early in the morning for horticulture class.

I exhale through my nose. "Well, at least there are no early mornings at the bar, Eva. We start your crash course tomorrow."

She squeals and hugs me. "You won't regret this. I promise, I'm going to be the best manager. And when you get back, we can talk about me staying on long-term."

I snort. "Let's not get ahead of ourselves."

17

KOA

Try as I might to convince Esther a motorcycle is the best ride for our trip, she insists we ride in a car with a roof. She's worried about rain. I'm worried about not getting to experience a wet Esther pressed against me in the rain.

I take her car in for a tune-up while she gives her sisters a crash course in bar management. I suspect her crash course is going to be pretty comprehensive, so I stop for supplies before I dip into the bar to referee.

The parking lot at Trader Joe's is bonkers, and by the time I grab a spot, I worry I have pissed off the dude in the tiny Honda gesturing at me. But then I recognize him. Another boyfriend of one of Esther's friends...

"Hey, man. I was trying to get your attention. AJ." He holds out a hand, and I shake it, eyeing him strangely as I'm not used to finding real adults out and about in the middle of a weekday. "I'm a teacher," he says with a shrug. "Summers off."

"Ah. And which Floof lady do you worship?"

He cracks a grin. "Samantha. And I wish I could say I

heard all about you, but I have no idea who you are really. It's quite the topic of discussion at our house."

We walk toward the store together, and he gestures for me to get a cart first. I guess I'm doing my shopping with another guy. A first for me, but if I'm honest, it's nice to have the conversation. I still don't quite know Esther's favorites, but I figure I can pick snacks for a road trip as well as the next fool. I swerve past the fruit initially but stop when I see that AJ is pining for the apples and cherries.

I gesture for him to lead the way. "I would have thought Piper activated a phone tree or something after yesterday."

He nods. "Oh, she did. I heard all about the Storm sisters and their issues. I'm going to help Eva, by the way. I teach science. I know she's interested in horticulture. I figure I have nothing else to do this summer."

"Is that right?"

He shrugs. "It's nice. I've been counting birds and looking for mushrooms. Tried to get Esther to use some foraged plants in her cocktail menu, but she wasn't into it."

"Gotta admit, that's probably sensible."

He tosses a bunch of lettuce in his cart, and I reach for a bag of carrots. I pretty much just push the snack aisle into my cart when we get there. I never met anyone who doesn't go wild for all the lentil crunches and veggie straws. AJ grabs a more modest selection of crisps and jogs toward the dairy case. I notice he's got a few boxes of cake mix, too.

Finally stocked up on yogurt, he turns to face me. "I'm glad you're forcing Esther to take a break. We all are. I know she's the most capable woman there ever was—apart from Samantha obviously."

"Obviously." I nod.

"Anyway, all these women are extraordinarily competent, and they do lean on each other...but Esther...she's always helping everyone else and never, ever leans on anyone."

I scratch at my chin. "She asked for help with the candles the other day..."

He laughs. "Right. Peeling labels of the holy Mary tubes. That's not actual help. If one of my middle schoolers can handle it, I say it doesn't count as a helping ask."

I sigh. "Well. We are indeed taking that road trip. So."

He grins. "I can't even picture her sitting in the car for the journey." He looks up at the ceiling. "I'm trying to think if I've ever even seen Esther sit...Sam sent me a pic of her getting a pedicure once..."

AJ and I finish up our shopping trip and he gives me his number, promising to connect me with "the other boyfriends," which gives me some small amount of pleasure. Even if Esther isn't thinking of me as anything but a temporary house guest, her friends have classified me as someone lasting.

My phone shakes in my hand, and I see I've been added to a group chat. FOOF DUDES. I scroll back through some of the messages, but it's mostly SOS calls to provide location information when the guys' girlfriends, or wives in some cases, have gone off-grid.

I don't think I've ever been in a group chat before. The teams I've coached have all used email listservs to communicate, and the lads will sometimes message me individually if there's a drink-up I should know about.

The chat lights up.

AJ

Hey guys, this is Koa's number. I found him today at Trader Joe's. The chocolate covered shortbread hearts are back, by the way. You're welcome for the hot tip.

UNKNOWN NUMBER (MAYBE: TED PRESTON.)

[fire emoji]

AJ

Guys, identify yourselves so Koa can add you to his phone. That fire was from Teddy. We probably won't hear from Cash for a while.

UNKNOWN NUMBER (MAYBE: CASH BRENNAN)

Yo. This is Cash. I'm on my way to the store to get chocolate cookies for Pipes. Don't call me later. I'll be busy being thanked.

AJ

How late is Ruby at camp today?

CASH

I've got 94 minutes left.

Um, hey. Koa here. Should I have bought Esther cookies?

TED

Yes. Go back to the store. Ply her with the dark chocolate buttery goodness.

AJ

Ditto Ted. Can say with 100% certainty they will be well received.

By the time I get to Bridges and Bitters, I'm worried my goodies will melt in the sun, so I lug the bags inside with me. The bar is closed, but the door is unlocked, and I press it open to find a row of dark-haired Storm sisters with notebooks. Esther must buy them in bulk. I always see her tucking the same little jotter in her back pocket.

Shit, thinking of her back pocket makes me want to stick my hand in there and squeeze. I set the bags on a table and clear my throat.

Esther whips her head around and smiles. And I'm already glad I went back to get the cookies, because when that fierce woman lets a smile slip, it's everything.

18

ESTHER

My sisters flock over to Koa like he's the Pied Piper. And he sort of is, brandishing huge bags full of snacks. They act like they aren't grown adults who could run out to the store at any time and buy their own food.

And then my own stomach gurgles, and I realize I didn't get myself anything for lunch, either. "Hey." He looks too damn good, smiling with those arms crossed over his chest. What's he always so happy about, anyway? He has no job, no family, and he, himself said he has no real sense of place. I'd be miserable if I didn't feel rooted here with all my sisters to take care of.

"I brought you something. It was meant to be for our road trip, but I guess we'll have to restock." He gestures at my sisters who have consumed an entire bag of chickpea onion rings, whatever those are. Eila is literally dumping the crumbs from the empty bag into her mouth.

Eva squeals as she reaches into the last bag on the table. "Oh MY god, these are the best cookies. Damn, Koa. You spoil us."

He looks panicked for a moment and reaches out for the bag. "Actually, um..." He drifts off and seems to try to compose himself. "Nevermind. Enjoy, girls." Eliza squints at Koa and then looks at the box of heart-shaped cookies. I've heard about these. Sam and Chloe call them orgasmic cookies. Piper violates her healthy eating rules for these.

Eliza smacks Eva's hand before she rips open the box. "Hold up, Eve. I think those are just for Esther."

Eva groans. "He told us to enjoy. I want one."

Eliza pinches our youngest sister who squeals and drops the box. Koa snatches out a hand and catches the cookies before they hit the floor. Eliza looks around the bar. "Hey, Storms. We've learned enough for one day, I think. I'm starving for actual food."

Eden and Eila groan in agreement and, the cookies mostly forgotten, grab their purses and wave as they head toward the door with promises to make sure Eva is here by four tomorrow. Eva, conversely, mutters about wanting the cookies.

"Eva don't be an idiot. They're sex cookies for Esther." Eliza shoves Eva, who stumbles and nearly trips out the door as my cheeks heat. Eva looks back over her shoulder at me, eyes wide. I stare at her, not sure what my face is doing as they all hustle out the front of the bar.

Koa clears his throat. "So, no expectations, but I did buy the cookies with you in mind." He grins again. "I ran into AJ at the store."

I laugh. "That explains the snack find. Thank you, Koa. That was very sweet."

"The cookies are sweet," he says, taking a step closer to me. "My intentions are nothing of the kind."

The air feels charged between us as I reach for the box. He presses it into my hand, his thumb stroking mine when we connect. We've been dancing around each other for days, not talking about how good it was between us the first time. The day we got married. The last time I saw him, five entire years ago.

I swallow, leaving my hand near his. He doesn't stop that movement of his thumb. "I...don't usually do repeats. Too messy."

He nods. "I don't usually, either. Never around long enough."

"So, I guess that settles that."

He inches closer to me. "Does it?" He stares into my eyes and doesn't look away, like he's trying to see inside me. I don't like it, but I am also spellbound under his gaze. I feel like I'm on display, but I also feel like I'm in safe hands, and this is something I'm not used to at all.

"How would it work?"

He smiles. Not a grin this time, but a lascivious, filthy smile. "You remember perfectly well how it will work, Esther."

I nod ever so slightly, flashing back to memories of him pulling my hair, shoving my shoulders into the mattress, tossing me around like I weigh nothing at all. And he's stronger now. Older, with more experience. "Oh god." The words escape my mouth with a shudder.

"It's just a few days, Wife. Then we part ways. Why not enjoy our honeymoon to the fullest?"

It's so hard to concentrate while he's talking this way. I should be doing so many things. Making more notes for Eva. Making lists. Placing orders in advance. I should be cleaning the bathrooms or changing out the kegs, but suddenly my body is propelled toward the front door of its own accord, flipping the deadbolt and pulling down the shade.

I am overcome with lust, and it's interrupting my ability to do anything else. I'm tired of fighting this attraction. I'm fully capable of having amazing sex with this man and not letting feelings get involved. I nod.

And then I walk back toward my hulking beast of a husband, wondering why on earth I've been avoiding this heft, those big thighs that dwarf my own. He reaches behind the bar and flicks off the lights, leaving us standing in a puddle of afternoon sunlight that pours through the transom.

"I want to feed you one of these cookies, Esther. See if they're really all they're cracked up to be."

"I'm sure they're fine." I am crowding his space now, feeling like this joining is inevitable. I watch, mystified, as one of my fingers traces along his chest. I hear a crackle and a crinkle and look up to see him offering me a heart-shaped chocolate treat.

"Open," he whispers, and when I do, he places the cookie on the edge of my lip. The dark chocolate is bitter-sweet and soft, and I nibble gently into the cookie, the flavor floods my mouth as he watches me eat. He feeds me the entire cookie while one hand snakes around my lower back, palm on my ass. I feel every hard inch of him, including the bulge at his crotch that I remember very, very well despite how drunk I was the first time I rode it.

"So, what's the verdict, Wife?"

I stare at his lips and then swallow, licking the corners of my lips to catch the remnants of the shortbread. "Delicious." I barely get the word out before he crashes his mouth into mine.

19

ESTHER

I'm drowning in sensation. Koa tastes like I remember and smells even better. His scent surrounds me as his arms envelope me, caging me in a strong embrace I know I could break free from...but would never choose to.

I feel his tongue spear into my mouth confidently, and he moans as I deepen our kiss. I hear groaning sounds I realize are coming from my own body as my hips begin to grind mindlessly, feverishly against his leg.

"You like that, eh?" He breaks the kiss and looks down as I press myself desperately against him, craving friction, and I gasp when I find some.

Koa's thigh is between my legs as he slowly walks us toward the bar. When my back hits the wood, he lifts me so I'm sitting on the edge of my own damn bar. "Poor Esther," he whispers as his hands jerk my thighs wide so he can stand between them. "Keeping her husband on the pull-out couch and denying herself a chance to feel good."

He grunts as he tugs on the hem of my tank, yanking it over my head in one motion while his other hand unfastens my bra with practiced ease. He takes a step back to stare at my exposed upper half, and I lean back on my hands, my chest heaving as my breath comes in rapid pants. Koa grins again, one finger tracing a nipple too gently. I hiss and then whimper when he pulls the finger back. "Come on," I growl while trying to pull him closer to me with my feet, struggling to sit upright from my position leaning back on the bar.

And then the fucker laughs, deep and low as he whips his own shirt off. "This is going to be slow, love." I feel like I'm on fire, like all I want is for him to plunge inside me and take the edge off, but all he'll do is lightly trace a nipple and stare at me like I'm a precious, precious thing.

"Koa, come on. I need..."

"What do you need, Esther?" He cocks a brow and doesn't stop tracing, alternating sides and then, blessedly, he gives one breast a squeeze.

"Just, fucking more!" I manage to lean forward and make contact with his skin, my teeth sinking into the golden flesh of his shoulder. At this angle, my nipples connect with his chest, and I squirm, needing him to touch me before I crawl out of my own damn skin.

Much too gently, Koa places the palm of his hand on my sternum and presses me back so I'm lying flat on the bar. I hook my legs around his waist, barely, and pull him against my center. I feel the length of his bulge and manage a few good thrusts through both of our jeans before his tongue connects with my stomach and I scream.

The heat and moisture both dissipate instantly as he trails a line down the soft dome of my belly, and I bury my fingers in his dark hair just so I have something to do. Koa unbuttons my pants, and I lift my hips for him as he starts to peel off my jeans and underwear. "That's a good girl." He plants kisses along each thigh once he has me stripped. I've never been exposed like this, spread out like a flight of whiskey. Just like a spirit connoisseur, he sniffs deeply and moans.

"So fucking perfect," he mutters, digging his fingers into the flesh of my thighs, then digging in with a bit more pressure, and I nod my head.

"Yes, please. More." I've lost all my words, all my ability to control the situation. I am a puddle of need on display for this man, and finally, eventually, much too slowly, he reaches between my legs and parts my folds with his thick fingers.

"Ah, Wife. You're very, very wet." He punctuates each syllable with a gentle flick of his thumb against my clit and to my horror, I almost come just from this light contact. I've spent way too many days thinking dirty thoughts about him as he slept on the sofa bed four feet from my head, all this muscle and bulk just a hair out of reach.

I hear a gentle thud as Koa drops his pants, and when I lift my head, I see him, naked and glowing as he runs his palms along my thighs. He kisses and licks at my stomach again, touches me everywhere except my quivering pussy.

I'm seconds away from struggling to sit up, leaping off this bar, and tackling him to the ground so I can hop on his dick and ride, but he senses my impatience and nods. "I've got you, Esther." And then he licks, long and deep, skewering me with that tongue of his. I moan, wanton, arching off the bar as he sinks his tongue inside me again and again.

"That's it, gorgeous," he purrs, pausing his licking to stroke and plunge with his thick fingers. One hand slides under me to palm my ass. "Come for me, Wife. I want to feel this wet heat pulse around me as you come for me."

And with a groan, I do as he commands. I come in a rush that takes me by surprise with its intensity. I come so long and so hard, waves crashing over me, and I barely notice him pull me from the bar, flip me over, and plant my feet on the ground. In my next breath I'm bent at the waist, tits pressed against the rounded edge of the boards while my husband's giant hands massage my ass.

"Christ, you're gorgeous. So peachy pink and round. I want to sink inside you and see you shimmer while I pound into you, Wife." As he mutters filthy things, Koa tears open a condom. I hear the crinkle of the wrapper, and then I feel the hot, huge head of him nudging at my entrance. I scoot my legs a little wider, arch my back, and then release a long "ahhh," as he sinks inside me.

"Yeah. That's right, Esther. We fit together so nice." He traces a hand down my spine and back up, gathering my hair in one hand. I brace my palms on the bar as he tugs on my ponytail, and then he begins to thrust in earnest.

This is what I've needed. This is what's been missing. This giant man bossing me around, spewing filthy words as he pounds into me. My ass jiggles with each thrust, and he mutters his appreciation. "Look at you. Look at your beautiful, rippling body taking every inch of your husband's cock."

I love how these words sound from his mouth, how his accent thickens the faster he fucks me. "Koa, god, please keep going. Holy shit. Yes." I press up off the bar with my palms, arching my back while he pistons his glorious dick in and out. I hear the sounds of us fucking, the slapping, wet connection, and it turns me on even more.

Just as I begin to fear my legs will give out, he wraps an arm around my waist. His teeth nibble my shoulder as he starts to stroke my clit. "I need you to come for me one more time, Wife. Come right now before I blast off inside you."

I nod my head and let it fall back on his shoulder. He squeezes me tight, and I feel the head of his cock twitch and expand. We come together, me screaming and him grunting into my ear. "Esther." He breathes my name as his breath slows, and I lower my head to the bar, exhausted.

Koa pulls out and hoists me upright, then lowers us gently to the ground where he grabs my jeans to use as a pillow. His wet cock lies on my thigh, and I stare at it, wondering how I will ever function again once we part ways at the end of the week.

And then he meets my eye and there is a look of such tenderness, such longing. I feel my blood freeze in my veins at the obvious intimacy in his expression, and he places a gentle, delicate kiss on my temple. I stiffen, unable to bear the vulnerability a second longer. I already bent the rules enough. I disentangle myself and get dressed, needing to finish my work.

20

KOA

Esther barely talks the rest of the day. After she blew my mind physically, she rushed to get dressed and told me she was taking the car back home, if I wanted a ride. As if I'd go an inch away from her after we just connected like that.

I can taste her on my lips and smell her on my skin the rest of the day, and it's torture lingering around the house while she scrubs the baseboards and rearranges her refrigerator—anything to avoid talking to me, sitting, or slowing down.

Eventually I get bored and decide to make myself useful, scouring the stove top and mopping the kitchen floor. All the sex and the cleaning and fretting makes me hungry, so I toss on a pot of rice and dig up some chicken from the freezer. I set that to cook low and slow in the oven while I go to town scrubbing grease from the microwave.

"What are you doing?" I peek beneath the microwave door where I've stuck my head to reach the back corners. I see Esther's bare toes wriggling on the floor beneath the hem of her jeans. Extracting myself from the microwave, I shake the bleachy rag a bit to emphasize my activities.

"Thought I'd join you giving the house a wipe." I smile at her, not because I'm trying to be coy, but because seeing her makes me happy. She's so damn gorgeous, statuesque, and confident. Except I am beginning to suspect the confidence is a front. Sure, Esther's competent, and she takes no shit from anyone. But I have a hunch she's that way because she's always had to be. From too young of an age.

And now she operates from this place where she always demands absolute and utter excellence, in all environments, but won't take a whiff of assistance to get there. She sniffs and peers over my shoulder into the microwave. She furrows her brow, like it's painful for her to admit I did a good job cleaning it. "Thank you," she mutters. "I've been meaning to get to that since someone heated up chili without a lid."

I nod. "Yeah, I scraped the red bits off first. The buttery puddle on the bottom was harder, if you'll believe it."

"That's what she said." Esther snorts and then claps a hand over her mouth, like she's appalled to be making bawdy jokes around me. Like I wasn't just balls deep inside her. And, thinking of that makes me hard again. I actually glance around the kitchen in search of a surface to bend her over, but she turns her head and sniffs. "Are you...do I smell...food? Are you cooking?"

"Ah. Right. I gesture at the pot on the stove. "I couldn't find a veg, but you had rice and enough stuff for a saucy chicken. Hope you like it hot." I wink at her and open the oven to peer at the meat.

"I can handle some spice." She looks around the kitchen, like she's disappointed there's nothing else for her to clean in here. "What can I do to help?"

"Finished scrubbing all the toilets then? Gone through the ceiling fans with a feather duster already?" I check her with my hip gently, and she swats at my arm.

"It's not like I get a ton of time to clean on days the bar is open. I like my space to look good."

I nod. "I can tell. And I think it's in great shape for your sister to destroy while we're away."

Esther growls. "She better not."

"Or what? You'll kick her out?"

Esther recoils from my words. "You know I wouldn't. She knows I wouldn't. Well. I think she does. Did she really think I'd toss her out for failing out of her class?"

I shrug. "Seems that way. I notice you didn't save any chores for Eva, though."

"Maybe I was going to have her scrub the microwave." She taps her toes on the ground, and I stare down at the dark polish. I'm surprised to see it there, I think. You have to sit still for nail polish, and I gather it takes a long time. I wonder who convinced her to take a pause and get her feet rubbed. Then I think about someone else rubbing her feet, and I feel my guts twist.

I shake my head. "You weren't going to have Eva clean the microwave now or ever, Esther Storm. You baby her." I poke her with my finger.

"Hey." Her voice is stern, her eyes spark daggers at me. "Don't talk to me about how I raise my sisters."

"That's just it, Wife. They're grown. They should at least clean up their own spilled food in the microwave."

She glowers at me. "Mind your own business, Koa." I shrug and bite back my comments about shitty roommates. I've had my fair share of those, and Esther isn't doing her sisters any favors by keeping them out of practice cleaning up their own messes.

The timer goes off for the rice, and I open the pot. A gush of steam hits my face, and I nod, seeing it's done perfectly. I reach around Esther for the butter dish and shake my head when I see crumbs in the butter, like someone scraped at it with a dirty knife. Esther sees and bites her lip, leaning back against the island while I stir some salvaged butter into the rice with a bit of salt.

She turns to the cupboard and gets a set of plates and glasses, stacking them on the island next to me just as my phone timer sounds for me to check on the meat.

"Everything's ready," I tell her, scooping out a few portions of the savory mix. I went a little heavy on the garlic, but I don't think it matters since it doesn't seem like I'm going to be waking up with my mouth near anyone's nose.

The silence while we eat is thick and awkward. Esther thanks me quietly for cooking and washes up her plate. "I'm heading to bed," she says, before it's even dark outside. By the time I clean up and head upstairs, she's asleep with her back to the sofa bed.

21

ESTHER

This is the longest I've ever spent with someone who has seen me naked. Other than my sisters, I guess. Not that I care who sees me naked because I look really fucking great naked. It's just…I don't do relationships. I don't do attachments. I spent all my affection dollars on my sisters, and I don't have a savings account where that's concerned.

So it pisses me off that I feel myself fretting about what Koa will do while I'm at the bar Tuesday. What do I care what he does? I haven't cared about what he's done for the past five years. I've barely given any thought to him at all, except for the occasional time I spot a guy who looks like he might be a Pacific Islander.

Anyway, I have way too much to do prepping my sister to manage the bar in my reluctant absence. I start to grow irritated that Koa and I can't handle this interview over video conference or something. It seems so restrictive that we have to haul ourselves to Philadelphia for this meeting when I live in a perfectly large city with perfectly functional government offices downtown.

"What crawled up your ass?" Eva startles me into dropping a metal pitcher of water, which she catches before it topples onto the floor from the back-bar counter. "I'd have thought those sex cookies would have put you in a better mood, sis. You're welcome, by the way, for me staying out late and giving you space for hanky panky."

"I don't need space," I mutter, scooping ice into the pitcher and setting it on a towel at the end of the bar. I've started putting out self-serve water and cups. People seem to appreciate pacing themselves, and I actually think business picked up a bit. Could just be the warmer weather. Sam would tell me to use her data tracking software, so I'd know for sure, but I haven't had time to set anything up yet.

"Go on and unlock the door..." I drift off in my instructions for Eva when I see that she's already smirking from the doorway. She propped open the front door, letting in a cool breeze and the afternoon sun. She also set out a sandwich board I've never seen before, advertising our seasonal cocktails. "Where'd that come from?"

"We spent last night crafting while you ate sex cookies." Eva dusts off her hands and smiles at the sign. "I think it looks nice."

"Knock it off with the cookies. I only ate one."

Eva arches a brow at me and frowns. "That was stupid. I'd eat an entire box of those sex cookies, if you know what I mean."

"Can you not talk about Koa that way?" I check the bottles on the speed rail to make sure our most common supplies are set up and ready to go. The tech startup crowd usually wanders in before five for an afternoon tipple before I think they go back to work to code things all drunk.

Eva laces a black apron around her hips and stuffs some ones from the register in the pocket. "Don't worry. I grabbed ten, and I'll remember to replace it." I frown. "I will. Esther, I've been studying. Look, I even laminated a cheat sheet."

She pulls a small deck of notes from the apron, laminated instructions for basic cocktails, reminders for how to close. I peer at the list, impressed that she didn't write down the combination to the safe. A very tiny screw loosens in the vault around my throat, and I breathe a bit easier seeing my sister is taking this so seriously. "The sign looks classy, Eva. That's a nice touch."

She shrugs. "It's a prototype. I wanted to see if drunkos trip on it or try and steal it before I invest in a nice one for permanent."

"You don't need to invest in anything for Bridges and Bitters, Eva. The bar generates money to pay for that stuff."

"Sure, sure. I just meant, when *we* invest." I try not to get rattled or scold her for assuming I'd ever share any ownership of my business with anyone. Before I can fret or say anything further, a group of young, bearded hipsters saunter in with a chorus of shouts for whiskey. We're off to the races.

"Whew, that was a lot." A few hours into opening, Eva leans against the back bar and fans herself with a towel. We've been going nonstop, but there's finally a lull between the after-work crowd and the pre-theater crowd. Her stomach growls. "Don't you have anyone coming in to give you a break? When do you pee?"

I shrug. "I just don't hydrate on weeknights." My sister's face contorts in horror, and I lick my bottom lip. I didn't mean to reveal that to her. "Honestly, when it's busy I don't really notice, and when it's dead I just sneak off and pee."

Eva glances at the few tables of customers, heads close together, chatting. "How often is it dead?"

I smile, proudly. "I guess it's not really."

Eva slaps her towel down on the bar with a thwap. "I'm not working alone while you're gone. That's nuts. Eliza can leave her goats unattended. Or maybe Eila should be here anyway, see how her hops are selling."

I wince. "I'm not carrying any of Eila's beers right now. They weren't big sellers."

Eva gasps. "Well...were you pushing them like you do your fancy cocktails? Maybe you need to market the beer better."

"My cocktails are the foundation of this business. It's called Bridges and Bitters. Bitters. Like with whiskey?"

Eva taps her chin. "I think I thought bitter was, like, for miserable people. To gather and drink!"

"Does this place look like a dive bar full of misery? My god, Eva. Wow." I know my sister is still a teenager, but does she really understand so little about my business? I opened this bar to be the opposite of a cheap bar selling shitty beer. That's the whole point, to come to a luxurious space and enjoy a delicate cocktail, carefully blended. To feel like everything is in its place, and every flavor has been considered. I hate that my sister doesn't see that.

"Hey." She puts a hand on my arm as I fuss around behind the bar, cleaning glasses and scrubbing cutting boards and knives in the sink. "What do I know? I'm sorry, Esther. Don't be mad."

I am mad. Maybe I'm not mad. I'm hurt, but I don't know how to explain this to my baby sister, so I sigh and look at her. "It's fine. And maybe you're right. I should hype up my kid sister's beer a little better."

Eva nods and reaches for the clipboard she stashed on a shelf. "So, I can put an order for a keg of her latest?"

I groan. "I was thinking we'd do bottles..." I hate working with kegs. I hate running to the basement to change them out, leaving the bar unattended. But there's definitely a higher profit margin and less risk of broken glass on my floor. Plus dealing with recycling is a pain in the ass. "Go ahead and order the keg. You're right."

Another group comes in the door, and we finish out the night in sync. Even I can admit Tuesday went a lot smoother with someone else here to help. We hadn't talked wages, but even considering Eva's pay for tonight, I made more than I normally would. I'll have to look into hiring more help. Eventually.

22

KOA

I've never been a meticulous planner. That should be obvious, considering my paperwork situation. But there's something about an impending road trip with Esther Storm that has me thinking about details I normally wouldn't. Like hotels. I never book them. Whenever I travel with a rugby team, we always crash with the guys.

I could ring up a rugby player in any city in the world and they'd offer me a couch. Been doing that for years in this country, but I know it's the same elsewhere.

It's just one of the things I love about the sport. Instant family. Worldwide. Just one of those things. The beach town I choose for our romantic interlude is one I know of because of rugby. There's a tournament there I've played in before, and I remember seeing a swanky hotel near the rat hole we piled into as a team.

As I search up hotels with posh bedding, I think about how rugby is not true family. Not like Esther's got with her sisters. Community, yes. But family? I try to push away the jealousy I feel at the blind loyalty those women show one another. Even when they're fighting, they know the other four will support them, hug them, and help them make things right.

I give Esther shit about babying her sisters, but if I'm honest, I'm jealous of that, too. One of the things I find irresistible about Esther is her extreme competence. She excels at everything, whether that's calming down an angry drunk, refinishing hardwood floors, or picking just the right drink for someone who's had a bad day. And all the while, she finds time to maintain a room for each of her sisters, even once they own their own business and live elsewhere. They've all got this home to return to. A hive, where Esther is the queen bee.

I don't want her to mother me like she does them, but I spent some quality time in her shower today thinking about what it'd be like to have her fold my laundry just the once.

I shake off those unhelpful thoughts and pick out a nice place in Asbury Park. I figure it's not too far past Philadelphia, and I can take Esther to the ocean before we sit for our interview. As I book a room with just one bed, I think about how I'll take her there, too.

Being with her yesterday was just as fantastic as I remember it years ago. I know she won't admit it, and I know she won't open up to me, but I let my curiosity get the better of me today, and I found her boxes in her closet when I went to stash my stuff. I saw her pile of notebooks full of drinks and dreams and a smaller box full of postcards I sent her, souvenirs I mailed her from all the towns where I've coached.

There's something between us, something more than paperwork, and I fully intend to take advantage of that chemistry while I can. To that end, I popped into a tiny shop today while I was running errands. I tidy up Esther's desk and make sure I have everything ready for when she rolls in after closing Bridges and Bitters.

A few minutes past ten, I light the candle and get busy putting away the sofa bed. I'm not staying there tonight. If I do my job properly, she'll be too tired to kick me out of her bed and too blissed out to notice that I'll sleep beside her, all those glorious curves pressed against me all night long. I grunt and shift around, my pants uncomfortably tight, when I hear the front door open.

Eva yawns loudly and makes a show of stomping up the steps and slamming her bedroom door. I grin and lie back on Esther's bed, hands behind my head, waiting. Even though I'm expecting her, I gasp when I see her in the doorway. The glow of the bedside table tosses a warm light onto her features and the candle flickers a bit as Esther registers the flowers on her nightstand. And then, of course, she frowns. "What's all this?"

"A bit of pampering for my girl." I pat the bed next to me as she drops her bag on the ground and kicks off her shoes.

"What smells nice?" She looks around, spots the candle, and tries to hide the pleased smile that tips just the corners of her mouth.

"Obviously, I do," I joke, giving my pits a sniff before patting the bed again more forcefully. She groans as she sinks onto the bed.

"I haven't sat all night."

I take hold of one foot and swing it up onto my lap. "I figured that was the case. Hence the candle."

"What's a candle got to do with—oh, god, that feels good." I start rubbing the ball of her foot, and she groans, melting into the bed. "How...candle...fuck, you're good at that, Koa."

"Mm hmm." I stare at her beautiful face as I continue to work on her foot. "Last season, the team I coached had a yoga teacher come to a training session. She showed the guys all this stuff to do to help the feet after a day of running about." I drag a knuckle down the center of Esther's foot and fold it as much as I can, watching her face melt in pleasure. "I figure working a bar in chunky heels does about the same damage as a rugby match."

"Candle, though?" Esther seems like she's about to fall asleep, a small smile now totally visible on those plump red lips.

"Ah. That's for your back. I'll show you in a bit. Other foot, Hun."

She slowly lifts her other leg into my lap, the abandoned foot a whisper away from my balls. I groan along with her as I start to work on her other foot, digging knuckles into the arch and stretching in between each of her toes. Once she's a puddle of relaxation, I release her foot and lean in to whisper. "Roll on your stomach, then, slide those jeans off, and let me really make you feel good."

She grunts, and I help her roll. "I can't tell if you're being dirty." She doesn't complain and eagerly unzips her jeans, giving them a tug over the roundest, most perfect ass in the world. I can't help myself, and I cup it with both hands, holding her cheeks in my palms and hoping the warmth of my skin feels nice while I compose myself.

"So," I start to explain. "The candle doesn't just smell nice. It's massage oil."

"I like how it sounds when you say massage."

"Massage." I repeat, reaching one hand for the jar and blowing out the flame. "I'm going to drip the warm oil on your back and then rub it in."

She stiffens a bit and turns, looking concerned. "Won't that burn? Hot oil?"

I shake my head. "Trust me." She bites her lip and tries to watch as I tip a bit of the liquid onto the small of her back.

"Oh." Her face shifts in surprise. "That feels so nice." I nod and pour a bit more of the oil, and she moans when I start to spread it on her skin. I scrunch her top up and slide my thumbs along her spine.

I have no training in this, and if I'm honest, I just want to keep my hands on her, to touch her as I ease her tension. I swing a leg around so I'm straddling her, and I know she feels my hard cock at her bottom as I push her top high enough to expose her shoulders.

Esther moans and sighs as I work, and I delight in every second. I move her hair aside and knead her skin, dripping more oil until it sets again. I put the candle back on the nightstand. "I could do this all night," I tell her truthfully, rocking my hips a bit to relieve some of the pressure as I luxuriate in her skin and curves.

"Please do." Her voice is muffled by her pillow, but she rocks her bottom a bit, wriggling until I know we're on the same wavelength for what comes next.

"You like when I take care of you?" I realize I don't just mean physically. I want to take care of her, of Esther. I change the way I'm touching her now, letting my fingers sneak around the sides of her body toward her tits. I trace a knuckle down her spine and then reach around her hip, not quite letting a finger brush against her mound. "You like when I make you feel good?"

I start to ease her underwear down, and she nods her head, moaning when I toss them across the room and nudge her thighs apart with my knee. "Ah, look at that. So wet for me. You *do* like being taken care of."

I dip a finger into Esther's folds, and she turns her head to catch my eye as I start to stroke her. She opens her mouth in a beautiful "oh," and starts to come around my finger.

23

ESTHER

"That's it, beautiful. You're gorgeous. I'm going to cherish you and make you feel so good." Koa keeps on fucking talking, spewing out words that should sound cheesy but absolutely do not after he's just spent, I don't know how long, rubbing and tweaking my body into a puddle of boneless mush.

I lie still as he peels off the rest of my clothes and massages me some more. I still can't believe how fast I just came for him, but it felt inevitable after he had his hands all over me, and I felt that monster cock of his pressing hard against my ass while he did it.

I forget to be angry at him for earlier, forget that I'm irritated to be thinking of him during my down time. I forget all my boundaries as I feel his glorious naked torso pressed hard against my back. Koa arranges my arms so they're over my head, flat on the bed, while my legs are spread open with him nestled between. He's big and solid, but so am I, and we fit together this way, his powerful frame capable of so much strength, but gently strumming my body with heated oil. Whose life is this?

I gasp when I feel his fingers back at my center. They're warmer this time, slick, and I can see that he's scooped a bit more soft oil from the candle. "Don't worry," he soothes. "I asked, and it's safe for intimate use as well as massage."

"There's that word again." I choke the words out as his thick, warm finger slides inside me so easily.

"Massage," he says again while he proceeds to do just that to my inner walls. A condom wrapper appears on the nightstand next to the snuffed-out candle, and I tense. As much as I like it from behind, I can never start out this way. I need a warm-up.

My breath comes fast and hard as he stretches me open and inserts a finger. Then another. "It's so good, Koa," I groan, and he whispers his approval. Since when do I seek a man's approval for anything?

"Good girl," he repeats. "Good, good girl." I feel the thick, blunt tip of him pushing into me. "Ah, that's it. Look how you just swallow me right up, Esther. My cock slid right into you." He grunts as I shove the pillow into my mouth to stifle my moans.

Koa presses his hands into my shoulders, continuing to massage me a bit while he drives me into the mattress. "That's right." The entire time he keeps talking, saying filthy things, and praising me for swallowing up his big, fat cock until I don't know what to think or do other than come again.

The delicious weight of my husband presses me into the bed until I'm cocooned from the inside and outside. He swells inside me and groans into my ear, nipping at the lobe as he comes, whispering my name and calling me his.

When he finally rolls off me, I stagger to the bathroom, drained from work and from relaxation and the fuck of the century. As I wash my hands, I look in the mirror and gasp to find him standing behind me, naked, dabbing at his junk with a huge grin on his face. Koa scrubs his hands and tugs my arm. He pulls me back to the bed and tucks me against him, spooning me.

I cannot allow this. This is a step too far. No. The massage and gentle sex was already too far. I don't have that kind of sex—tender, romantic. And I don't fall asleep cradled in a lover's arms while he runs his fingers through my hair, humming to me. I don't do that.

I WAKE up still pressed against Koa, my hair still woven through the fingers of one of his hands while the other huge arm lies heavy around my middle. I stare down at the tattooed muscle, noticing for the first time that the flowers are similar to those inked on my own arm. My tattoo is silly. Sentimental, really. A bird nestled on four flowers...because I'm like a mama bird to my four sisters. I wonder if they know that's why I got it, or what they think about that if yes.

I trace the edges of Koa's botanical tattoo. The flower is different.

"It's a poroporo," he says into my ear. I glance over, but his eyes are still closed. He snugs his arm, pulling me closer.

"I thought Māori guys have those swirly tattoos." I keep tracing the petals of his flowers, and he purrs like a manly cat.

"Want to get it in New Zealand," he says, sleepily. "They tell a story. I want to do it right."

I roll to face him, a difficult feat with him gripping me so tightly. And I'm not sure what makes me say it, but I feel my mouth forming the words, "I want to go with you." And I mean it, and that terrifies me. I regret the words immediately, for all they represent, for all the logistics involved in making them real, for all I'd have to let go and trust to make it happen.

Koa cups my face with his big hand, and I feel safe again, calm. "That'll be nice."

Abruptly, he smacks my ass and bites the tip of my nose. "Up you get. We're on the road in an hour."

He springs from the bed and stretches, his morning wood at my eye level in all its brown, uncircumcised glory. I resist the urge to flick it when he practically skips into the bathroom and cranks on the shower. I stare at the ceiling and listen as he whistles.

24

KOA

"For the last time, Esther, I learned to drive in this country. Yes. I drive on the correct side of the road." Esther stands on the curb nervously rubbing at her scarf. She's come up with every reason in the world not to leave for this trip and still won't own up to being nervous about leaving the bar for a few days.

I lean toward her from the driver seat of her own car. "Do I need to throw you over my shoulder and haul you into the back seat? Because you know I will. And I'll enjoy it."

She flushes and steps into the car. From the front door, I hear a round of applause as Chloe, Piper, and Eva cheer. Chloe shakes her phone around, and I can see a few more of Esther's friends are on video chat celebrating her departure.

Piper whistles. "Don't even think about us while you're gone."

"You're gonna have that beachy hair I told you about!" Eva runs her fingers through her own dark locks as Esther flips them all the bird and slams her door. She stares straight ahead.

I wave at the send-off crowd and blast the horn a few

times before I start us out heading east. Esther is quiet until we're on the highway, when she bites her lip and waves at the approaching toll sign. "I don't have one of those pass things. Do you have cash? I don't even have cash. What do people do when they don't have wads of tips in their pants pockets?"

I squeeze her thigh and keep on driving. "Relax, boo. They stopped doing cash tolls a few years back. They just take a picture of your license plate now and send you the ticky."

"Hmm." She frowns at me. "Where have they been sending your *tickies,* then?"

I cluck my tongue. "I always take the scenic route when I'm on the bike. Lie low, enjoy the view. Everyone wins."

Esther leans her elbow on the window and shifts so she's staring at me. "You've been that far off the grid for that many years? When you don't have to be?"

I shrug and veer right, following signs for Philadelphia even though we've got hundreds of miles to cross before we get there. "It's not so bad. Thank you for handling all the insurance premiums, by the way. Not that I had to use it at all. Nice to have a backup."

Esther's right that I have the right temporary paperwork to be here without fearing that a highway toll will get me deported. It just always seemed best not to poke the bear, especially when the immigration office was backed up so long and kept postponing our interview.

"So, you never get sick, either?" She licks her lips and looks around for the stash of snacks and drinks. I point to the back seat and admire the view, carefully from my side vision of course, as she stretches back to grab some things.

"Can't very well be down with an illness when I'm leading the teams, can I?" I tap at the steering wheel.

"Anyone else on the team we can replace, but the coach signs the check for the referee."

Esther laughs. "You could use the off-season for pneumonia and whatnot."

"Nah." I grin and flick her arm. "It's always warm enough for rugby somewhere."

"I don't know how you stand it, not knowing where you'll be every quarter. Having to get used to new smells and people and their habits all the time."

"You telling me you're not getting used to people's smells every day of the week? What two days are the same at your place of business, then, Wife?"

She nods her head. "Fair, fair. It's not quite the same, though, is it? I mean I go home to the same bed every night. Yell at the same sisters in the morning."

I'm quiet for a beat, and Esther starts picking at her scarf again. "Maybe if I had sisters, it'd feel different."

"Well, you've got four of them for another few weeks at least." Esther winces as soon as she says it and then shakes a bag of crisps at me to try and change the energy in the car. "Where did you find ketchup flavored chips, anyway? I never even heard of those."

"That row of shops where I got the massage oil? They have an international market. I got all kinds of stuff. Wait till I show you the Hokey Pokey I found!"

Esther opens her mouth to say something about the old timey dance with the same name, but I cut her off. "It's a Kiwi treat. Haven't seen it in years. I almost cried when I got a packet of it. Ate half right there in the parking lot, but I saved the rest for us when we get to the shore."

Esther eats a few crisps, staring at me skeptically. "You planned this whole thing out pretty well."

"One of us had to! Not like you left me much else to do

after I scoured your whole kitchen." She punches me in the arm, and I laugh. I like messing about with her, joking. I open my mouth, and she inserts the perfect amount of crisps. I try not to think about how well we work together.

She doesn't do relationships, and neither do I. But the longer I spend with my on-paper wife, the less appealing it seems to take off into the sunset at the end of this thing. But what would I do if I stayed? Change my entire life?

"I don't even know what it'll feel like to be settled," I say before I forget not to say such things out loud.

"You mean the paperwork?"

"Yeah. I've been in paperwork limbo for longer than I ever had stability I think."

"Tell me again why your parents let all that slide?"

I stare ahead and change lanes to pass a lorry moving slow. "Mum wasn't sure they'd stay here at first. Turned her nose up a bit at the culture...but Dad loved it here. And the university was good to them. Excellent life insurance policy, as it turns out."

Esther groans. "I never know how to respond when you make jokes like that about such awful tragedy."

I tap on the steering wheel again. "I guess you could joke right back at me. 'I see you've spent it well, Koa,' that sort of thing."

"The only thing I can see you've spent on, is me." She purses those red lips, and I can't help but reach out to rub a thumb down her cheek.

"Like I said, I spent it well."

25

ESTHER

When Koa and I switch drivers along the turnpike, I realize that I haven't driven on the highway for any significant length of time in years. The intermittent hum of my cell receiving texts reminds me that I'm never really in a position where I can't answer it...like driving on the highway. I think I drove to West Virginia for a special order of moonshine once when I first opened the bar, but I really don't leave Pittsburgh.

Ever.

"Do you have directions for where we're headed? Or do I just stay on the turnpike until it ends?"

Koa drums his palms against the dash. "End of the road, lady. Just keep going east." And then he winks. And then he offers me a sex cookie.

"I thought we ate all those the other day." God these cookies are amazing. I definitely see why my friends have branded them this way.

"Esther. Doll face. You ate one cookie before I bent you over that bar and made sure you enjoyed it."

I gasp at his words and choke a bit on the cookie crumbs. "Shit, Koa." I turn up the blower on the air conditioner and regret it as the central Pennsylvania fertilizer aroma seeps into the vents. "Ugh. I need another one of those cookies to calm down from the first one."

The second one he hands me is soft and warm from the box being on his lap. No wonder I need the air on so high. The man radiates heat. He's so...comfortable, splayed out in my car as best he can given the space constraints.

"Should we prep for the interview questions? Get our story straight?" I wash the second cookie down with a swig of water. The closer we get to Philadelphia, the more it hits me that there are real stakes here for him. And me, I guess. I've avoided looking up the consequences for me if things don't go well. He smiles.

"We did all that. You run the bar. I travel for my job. We're madly in love and met at that dive bar where you were always snippy with me after class."

"I wasn't snippy."

"Keep telling yourself that, darling. And hey, I don't blame you. All those college-aged lads and lassies coming in, making a pass at you, tipping for shit." He drapes an arm around my shoulder, and I stiffen.

"Not while I'm driving. Come on." I am midway through passing a tractor-trailer before he pulls himself back onto his own side of the car.

"And the lasses don't need to make passes at me." I smile at him. "Men work too hard for bartenders' attention. It's boring and predictable."

"How many of them made you offers of marriage, though?"

"Only you, Koa."

"Ah, so I'm un-boring then? Is that a compliment?" He shoves a cookie in his mouth and slides the box back into the insulated bag along with the untouched carrots and grapes. I know he can't possibly binge carb snacks like this all the time and maintain muscles like that, but it's nice to eat trash food and do something totally out of the ordinary.

A little nice.

"Seriously, though, do I have to watch for a turn or something? I don't want to be driving through Philadelphia at rush hour."

He pulls up his phone and clicks around for a bit. "All right. There are two turns between here and the hotel."

"You made hotel reservations?"

"You wound me, babe. I couldn't risk them running out of king-size beds and sticking us with two doubles. Imagine? All that space between me and your lovely bottom..."

I can't help but laugh at his antics. He's very frank about his attraction to me, and normally I'm that way, too, with someone I'm fucking. But this has been almost two weeks straight of the same person, and things get more intense each time, more intimate. It's a lot.

"You've got another hundred miles before we hit I95, and I can take over driving when that happens."

WE SPEND the next few hours teasing each other, eating snacks, and singing Bruce Springsteen songs to prepare for New Jersey. When we finally get to the beach town, Koa heads right past the hotel. True to his word, he drives east until the road ends. "Here we are, then." He unbuckles and leaps out of the car.

I hesitate, suddenly aware of how dumb it is to be 30 and never having seen the ocean. What's wrong with me, that I never, ever, leave my city? When I open the door, I hear gulls screeching overhead, and I can smell the sea. I don't know how I know that's what it is, but there's an unmistakable salt scent everywhere.

As I climb out of the car, I accept Koa's hand. He pulls me close and shuts my door behind me. "Are you ready?" I shake my head, and he laughs. "You can do it. I'm here if you swoon and collapse."

I can always count on him to lighten the mood, I'm learning, so I give his hand a squeeze and follow as he heads toward the boardwalk. We keep going until I freeze and look right ahead.

The sea is nothing like the Great Lakes. This is nothing like the three rivers I see every day in Pittsburgh. This is massive and powerful, and I stare and stare as the waves crash onto the beach.

"This is high tide," Koa whispers. I look up to see he's moved behind me, wrapped both arms around me, and rested his chin on my head. We stand in the middle of the boardwalk as I watch the ocean.

"Where is everyone?"

I feel him shrug. "It's early in the season, and it's not quite five. They're probably all at work." He doesn't push or twitch as I stare my fill, and when I finally move to walk closer, he slithers his hands from my hips until his fingers twine into mine.

And I allow it. I let him squeeze my hand as we descend the steps to the sand. I let him kneel in front of me and slip off my shoes, and I watch as he kicks off his own until we are both barefoot on the beach.

"You ready now? To feel the pull of Moana?" I nod, ever so slightly, and feel the way the sand gets wet and firm the closer we get. Eventually, the cold foam licks at my toes, and I brave another step closer.

We stand, hand in hand, as the waves crash on my ankles. Eventually, I realize I'm crying.

26

KOA

When Esther's teeth start clattering, I convince her we should head to the hotel and check in. "We can come back to the beach as much as you want. With sweatshirts."

"I thought you call them jumpers?"

"Nah. Here, I'll drive." I usher her into the car, and she reaches for her cell phone. She frowns at the screen.

"I missed 85 text messages."

"How is that possible? Let me see." She angles the screen toward me, and I see a slew of texts from her sisters, from her friends. As Esther scrolls through the chaos, I feel a bit better seeing that a lot of them are just one-word texts from a very excited Eva.

Open for business!

I

Mixed

A

> Martini!!!!!!!!!!!

A dozen or so more are from Samantha, Nicole, and a bunch of other women Esther has labeled in her phone as "Foofers."

> SAM
>
> My martini is so strong. Please never come back.

> SAM
>
> Just kidding. Your sister did great.

> NICOLE
>
> Eva does NOT have your knack for mocktails. What should I drink?

> CHLOE
>
> Esther, don't worry about our mocktails. Enjoy your time at the beach.

> NICOLE
>
> Fuck that. I want something pretty to drink like you made for Orla!

I arch a brow at Esther as she scrolls rapidly through the messages, clearly searching for anything actually important. "Do they always do this?"

Esther shakes her head. "Well, no. I'm usually there mixing them the drinks, aren't I?"

"But, on a regular day, how many times do people interrupt you with this sort of information?"

"It's not an interruption. They're my friends. And my sisters."

The phone pings in her hand, and I can see this one is from Eila. It's a picture of Eva with her tongue out in concentration as she pours whiskey. Esther groans. "That's the expensive stuff. I hope it's for someone who plans to pay."

I reach for the phone and slide it to silent, then stick it in my shirt pocket. "Let's just let it be while we get settled."

Esther nestles her head against the headrest and shivers again. I turn on the car and crank the heat, wishing I could wrap myself around her instead. "Right," I mutter. "Hotel."

I went a little overboard and splurged for the Asbury Hotel because they do rooftop movies, and I want to sit up in the breeze as Esther leans against my chest while we watch something romantic. Obviously, we needed an ocean view, so I figured why not book the panoramic suite with the walk-in rain shower? I start to drool thinking of all the things I can do with Esther in there.

I ease the car up to the valet stand and nearly growl when the attendant opens my door before Esther's. Seeing my expression, he scurries around the car to my wife. But then I actually growl when he offers her a hand. I didn't think I had it in me to feel jealous. The realization sets in with unease as I think about the implications. I care enough about Esther to mind if another person hits on her.

I work pretty hard to keep things casual with the ladies, ever since my parents died. I don't know if I have it in me to recover from heartache again. Since when am I catching feelings for Esther Storm?

I drag a hand down my chin as I wait for the valet to pull our bags from the back seat and onto the luggage cart. I need to watch myself. I look around all the modern grandeur of this ridiculous gesture and chastise myself for getting so involved.

What did I really think was going to happen after we settle things with my paperwork? I'm just going to ride off like I always do. I haven't stayed in one place since university, and I only did that to bide time while I could rely on a student visa.

Esther smiles at the valet and reaches in her pocket for cash but remembers she doesn't have any and frowns. I fish out my wallet and hand the guy a bill without looking as I place my other hand on Esther's back to guide her toward the front desk.

"Koa Stewart," I tell the concierge. "My wife and I are checking in."

27

ESTHER

"I've never seen anything like this." I drop my purse and stride over to the window. Or, rather, one of the massive windows since there are two entire walls of glass looking out at the ocean. Sure, it's a block away, but honestly you need that much distance to appreciate the enormity of it. "I just...never appreciated how small I am. If that makes sense?"

Koa leans against the wall by the door with his arms crossed over his chest, a strange expression on his face. "Yeah. Makes sense." He pushes off and walks over to stand next to me, leaning his forearms on the window to gaze into the distance. "I think a lot of people think deep thoughts when they're looking at the ocean."

I rest a palm on his arm. "Thank you." I drum up as much sincerity as I can blend with kindness. It's all a bit foreign for me. "Thank you for bringing me here. This is..." I gesture around the room, noticing the walk-in shower with a bench and raising my eyebrows. "This is really freaking nice."

"Only the best for my Esth...er."

I nudge him with my shoulder and laugh. "Goof." I look around the huge space, at the table and chairs by one row of windows, at the bed nestled in the corner. At the light fading as the afternoon wears on. "Are you hungry?"

"Always."

I press a hand to my stomach. "I should have gotten a sandwich or something, but I was so into all our snacks on the road."

Koa grins. "The sea air makes everyone hungrier. It's a whole thing." He squeezes my hand. "Do you want to change or just grab a sweater and head out?"

"Sweater is fine." I drift over toward my bag and hoist it up on the bed to unzip it. I stashed my sweater right near the top and— "What the hell?" I scowl at the contents of my bag, which are totally different from the things I packed this morning. I'm about to tell Koa that the bellhop brought up someone else's luggage when I recognize Samantha's scrawl on a note stuffed into something lacy.

"You're welcome. And don't worry about the bar."

Digging around in futility, I see that Samantha and unnamed assistants have swapped out all my jeans and turtlenecks for clingy dresses, lingerie, and...

"Is that a bikini?" Koa appears behind my shoulder, and I slam the suitcase lid shut, not wanting him to see. I whip around to face him, and his eyes are molten. "You brought a bikini?"

I can't very well tell him my bag is stuffed full of sexy things, so I nod rapidly. "I thought we could hot tub." I groan as I say it because the thought of being in a hot tub wearing just a bikini while Koa sits beside me wearing just a pair of shorts...

"Yes," he breathes. "Yep." He looks around. "Where's

your sweater? I want to feed you and then defile the hot tub."

I dig down to the very bottom of the bag, praying my friends took mercy on me and thought of cool evenings. I sigh when I find something fuzzy. It's a bright blue scarf-type thing, and I can't tell if it's meant to be a poolside coverup, but I decide it'll work just fine for warmth. I wrap it around my shoulders. "Let's go."

I bend to get my purse and phone, but Koa shakes his head and plucks the phone from my hand. "I want you all to myself." He yanks open the bedside drawer and stuffs the phone in with the hotel Bible.

I swallow, realizing that I also want him all to myself this evening. I'm not used to the vulnerability of that, of wanting someone. Of wanting them to want me.

Not for sex. I know I'm amazing at that. And Koa most certainly wants me in that way. But he also wants my undivided attention, and he wants to hear my thoughts about the sea, and he got me this beautiful room so I could be surrounded by ocean views when I got too cold to stand with my feet in the actual waves. He's forcing me to think about my own needs...and I'm a person who barely listens to my own bladder, let alone my desires.

"Gah. This is too much."

He smiles. Not one of his grins, but a real smile. A knowing, truly happy smile. A smile full of gentleness and...devotion. "Let's just get a burger and talk. You can make fun of my accent."

"Will you be getting chips with yours?" He nods, and I tug my scarf a bit tighter as we walk out the door. "And will you put ketchup on them?"

He shakes his head. "Absolutely not. Heathen." Koa drops a kiss on the top of my head as we wait for the elevator. And just because we're on vacation, and it's pretend, and there's nobody here who knows me to see and make a big deal...I sigh contentedly and lean against that big, sturdy chest. I let him wrap an arm around my shoulders and guide me across the street.

To a bowling alley.

He rubs his palms together. "This'll do nicely, eh? Should we make a bet for who wins?"

28

KOA

I've always known Esther's more of a burger gal than "grain-free Asian fusion" type of fancy grub. Toss in a bowling match where I could watch her bend over again and again in those tight jeans? I'm already the winner.

Regardless of the way I've been careless with my feelings the past week, I will never, ever turn down the opportunity to watch a gorgeous woman with a generous backside bend over.

Bowling turns out to be a fantastic idea because whatever hesitation was wrinkling her brow earlier is totally gone as she skids around in those ridiculous shoes. We splurged and each bought a pair of socks with the bowling alley's logo. "It'll be a souvenir," she insisted, stuffing my white athletic socks in my shorts pocket.

So here I sit, eating chips, joyfully watching my wife toss a gutter ball, when I hear some bloke shout my name. I always turn when I hear "Koa Stewart!" Because, frankly, there aren't any other Koa's in this country. It's always me.

Esther hears the shout and whips her head around, too, and we both stare as an entire rugby team shoves into the bowling alley, kitted out in matching polo shirts. "Hey, Dozer." I stand up and grasp hands with my old mate, tugging him against my chest and sharing a back pat. "What brings you lot across the Mississippi?"

"Sevens in the Sand, man. Hey, you want to join? We could use another sub."

I scratch the back of my neck. I should have checked the date of the tournament before I brought Esther here. So much for quiet walks holding hands with her, talking about our plans for the future. *Future.* I pause, realizing that part of me dreams of having a future...with Esther. I've been going above and beyond for her because I can see myself *always* giving a bit extra for Esther. I realize I'm irritated that the lads are infringing on my trip with her because I want to focus on this woman.

Rugby tournaments bring large athletes, raucous crowds, and (especially beach tournaments) bonfires. Esther presses against my side, and I tuck an arm around her waist without thinking. It feels natural and necessary to touch her whenever I can.

Dozer squints. "Who's this, Stewart? You still got a gal in every port?"

Esther frowns, and I want to punch my former team-mate. "Easy, man. This is Esther Storm." I want to shout our marital status from rooftops but decide to follow Esther's lead on the matter. Her eyes sparkle, and she clenches her teeth. Is it too much to hope she's irritated to come into contact with my past behavior? She doesn't assert herself as my wife, so I just give her a squeeze and tip my chin back toward our lane.

"I wish I could join you for the match, mate, but we're only in town for a few days."

Dozer shrugs and the other guys start passing around

bowling shoes. There are only so many pairs of the largest size shoe, so they decide they'll have to share and take turns. I huff out a laugh seeing them walk around in their socks as they choose bowling balls from the rack.

"Hope you'll at least stop by and watch for a bit. Esther, there's a women's side, too. If you're looking for something to do." Dozer waggles his brows, and Esther twitches her nose.

"We'll see." She walks back to our seats, and I follow her.

"Sorry about that. I should have checked if there were events in town."

"Gal in every port?" She crosses her arms.

I take a bite of my burger and chew for a bit. "From what I hear, you have a gal on every bridge."

She sighs and slumps a bit in her chair. "You're right. I'm being a hypocrite."

I snatch a chip from her plate, and she swats at my hand. "But you're a wee bit jealous, eh?" I wink at her. "It's a good look on you."

"I don't know. It's weird, I guess. Seeing other people who know you, hearing what they know about you."

"I've spent the better part of a fortnight surrounded by people who know you intimately, Esther. They all know you're amazing."

She taps at her lip and stares over at the rugby guys, swapping shoes and high fives. "Maybe you should play. Let me see you being amazing."

I shake my head. "Didn't bring my kit."

She laughs. "Oh, because lack of shoes seems to stop those guys." I scratch the back of my neck and watch the lads. Then I remember the sand tournament is all played barefoot anyway. If I can borrow a jersey from them, I could probably get away with playing in my swim trunks.

"You really want to spend your beach time watching a bunch of idiots knock heads?"

Esther leans closer to me. "Muscled athletes running around on the sand? Men and women? With the ocean as a backdrop? Can't think of anything better, Koa."

We finish our match, forget to keep score, and I swap numbers with Dozer, getting the details for the tournament the next day. Esther inserts herself at my side as we sit with the lads. She laughs as they share their rugby nicknames—crap like Leggy and Meatwad, Cyclops and Nipples. "Why don't you have a weird name?" Esther peers up at me with those wide eyes, and all I can do is shrug.

In truth, I've never stuck around a team long enough to earn one. I didn't have health insurance in university after my parents passed, so I couldn't play. And once I married Esther, I only stuck with each team for a season. By the time I'd do something stupid enough to potentially earn me a nickname, I'd be moving on to the next city.

"What would my nickname be? If I played rugby?" She intends the question for me, but Dozer slaps the table emphatically.

"Stormy. No question. That's a kick-ass last name. Plus, you're probably fierce on the field."

Esther chews on an ice cube from her soda. She's not drinking tonight, and I can't tell if it's because she doesn't approve of the bartender or she's trying to avoid thoughts of bars altogether for her own sanity. "I don't play sports."

Dozer clutches at his chest in mock horror, but I give Esther's shoulder a squeeze. "Ah, but she owns a bar. Which makes her the most important member of any rugby team, right boys?"

There's a resounding murmur of agreement, with exchanged promises to invade her bar if the team ever passes through Pittsburgh. I don't have the heart to tell any of them there's already a rugby bar on the south side of the city. Instead, I bask in the glow as she comes up with a custom cocktail for their team on the spot—something with rum and citrus.

"What about half-time oranges? Is that a thing? I swear I've heard my friend Chloe talk about sucking on oranges at half-time in soccer."

"Sweetheart, you can't say sucking and not expect me to drag you back to our hotel room." I whisper into her ear, feeling filthy and turned on as she shoos me away.

Leggy and Cyclops nod enthusiastically. "That's right. Half-time oranges in the heat. Perfection."

Esther procures a tiny notebook from her pocket, and I marvel that I didn't notice the outline of it in those tight pants. I smile, recognizing her signature tiny jotter. Esther nods, and I smile as she makes notes. "Rum, orange juice, some seltzer...what about coconut water? I see that in all those fancy ass sports recovery drinks now."

I wince. "It'd be chewy..."

Leggy leans forward excitedly. "No, man, it's good. That Prime stuff is amazing. You're on to something, Stormy."

She beams. "Half-time orange with dark rum, orange juice, seltzer, and coconut water. Not coconut cream or whatever's in a Painkiller. This will be different." She snaps her notebook shut and grins. "When you come to Bridges and Bitters, I'll have a whole pitcher for you and the rest of the Mountain Sloths. Is that really your team name?"

By the time Esther and I head back across the street to our suite, she's happy and swaying as she holds my hand. "I haven't thought up a new drink in a long time," she admits. "I've been so busy with everything..."

"You mean solving everyone else's problems?"

She shakes her head. "No. I mean hosting Chloe's party and all the stuff with Eva at school and..." She stops in the doorway of our hotel. "Those *are* everyone else's problems. You're right."

I nod. "I know it, Stormy. I'm always right. I feel like we mentioned this before..."

I laugh as she swings at me and, despite the crowd in the lobby, I heave her over my shoulder and make my way toward the elevator as she kicks and squeals in delight. I don't care who sees me hauling my wife away like a cave man. Even before I play in any tournament, I know I'm the winner here.

29

ESTHER

I can tell Koa regrets using my phone as our alarm for the morning because it chirps and vibrates almost constantly. This is the longest I've been away from my sisters in years and, considering I only met my Foof friends after I got married, this is the longest I've ever been away from their collective energy.

I know most of the messages are group chat gossip or FYI notes about the bar. But I can't help checking immediately because my heart never quite lets go of the worry things are amiss. I spent too many years with things amiss.

I like to joke that scrounging for food helped put hair on my legs, but the truth is I was on watch for years. On watch is my natural state, waiting for the catastrophe, preparing to intervene. I can negotiate with the sternest medical billing clerk on behalf of my sisters, and I can stretch a bag of flour and a stick of butter like you wouldn't believe.

But I can't sleep in on vacation.

So I lie in our massive room as the gauzy curtains dance in the air conditioning. I steep in the warmth of Koa's skin as he hugs me tight and groans each time another text message beeps on the nightstand. And then the alarm goes off, just as the sun pops onto the horizon where I can see it rising above the sea.

"I'm going to hurl that mobile into the ocean if you don't turn it off, Esther."

I stretch contentedly in the bed as he stands and stretches next to it. Naked, he twists and cracks his back, and I reach a finger for his golden muscles. Tan and smooth, he seems to glow in the sunrise. I can take a minute to appreciate this view. And I do. I stare my fill and smile, knowing that if I were the type of person who indulged in fantasies, I'd dream of staying here with him forever.

Koa kisses the top of my head, still naked. "You going to leave that cursed thing here in the room while you come watch me play?"

I arch a brow at him. "You seriously going to tell me what to do?"

He laughs. "Be a good wifey and watch me play. No distractions." He tugs on a pair of swim trunks and a t-shirt. "Please?"

I roll my eyes at him. "I need the phone to pay for my coffee. Don't throw cash at me. I like the tap and go." He squints, considering. "I tip with cash," I admit.

With a shrug and another kiss and a promise to keep the phone tucked away, Koa heads out to find the rugby guys. I follow his advice and take my time. I skip the shower, hoping we'll take one together later, and I force myself to read the entire menu in the cafe downstairs, even though I know I'll be getting coffee and a bagel.

I've heard things about New Jersey bagels. Everyone swears there's something in the water here that makes the dough so special. I'm not about to miss my opportunity. And then I make my way to the beach, where it takes no time at all to locate the rugby tournament.

Shirtless men are everywhere, regardless of physique. Koa mentioned to me that rugby is a sport for everybody, and I'm pleased to see it's true. There are thick athletes and lanky ones. Even on the women's teams, there are round bodies and lean ones, tall and short. Everyone seems to have a role to play, and even though I don't know the rules, I nestle into a beach chair eager to watch all this action come together.

Koa's group is gathered on the sidelines, watching a women's match finish up. I like seeing him watch the players. I wonder what he's thinking and know he's taking it all in as a coach. This is his version of assessing the client and choosing the perfect drink, I decide.

But then my husband takes the field, and I am pretty sure I stop breathing. Koa Stewart is, in a word, magnificent. He cradles the ball like a precious object, and it seems to sail from his fingers perfectly when he passes it to a teammate. Then, no matter how wild or frantic the pass, his big hands manage to find that ball and snatch it from the air.

He barrels down the sand faster than a man that large ought to be able, and the other team literally bounces off him rather than bring him to the ground. I let out a cheer as he dives across the tape marking the...do they call it a goal zone? Anyway, he obviously scores, and his teammates clap him on the back before quickly running back to get themselves situated, and do it all again.

Koa is so comfortable playing rugby, which seems weird to think since I can tell the other men are physically jarring him as they try to bring him to the sand. Nobody wears pads or helmets. The game is a crush of bodies coming together. At one point, there's a group of players right near where I'm sitting, and I can hear them all grunting with the effort of moving down the sand.

I'm shocked when the referee blows the whistle, and the match has ended. It seemed to go by in an instant. I didn't even finish my breakfast, but that's mostly because I couldn't peel my eyes away from the action.

I watch as Koa chugs a bottle of water—I hope it's water after all that running in the sun—and he peels off his shirt, handing it to the guy, Dozer. And then, topless, muscles glinting, he beckons me toward him. And I go, drawn to him, not caring that I'm responding to the beck and call of a man.

"That was amazing," I whisper as he pulls me in close. He's gritty with sand and smiling. He smells like sunscreen and sweat.

"You liked that? Your first rugby match?"

I nod and he kisses my neck, just below my ear, sending rays of needy pleasure through my body. "We've an hour before the next time we play. Sit with me and watch the competition?" He tugs me onto his lap on a low chair in the sand, beneath a canopy the team has brought. Koa murmurs into my ear as he watches the games in progress, muttering about poor timing and finding space.

"That's the way, lass," he whoops as a woman catches an errant ball with one hand and streaks up the side near where we're sitting. Sand flies in the air from her bare feet as she runs. I never really understood the appeal of exercise when Orla and Nicole and Chloe gush about sports. But now, seeing this woman's facial expression, the power, focus, and then utter delight when she scores...I almost want to cry I'm so moved by the whole thing.

"God, I miss coaching," Koa says, patting my thighs with gusto. "The only thing better than scoring is watching players score, knowing the steps they took to get there. Knowing they took my advice." He whoops again and sighs.

I stiffen. "So, you'll be looking for another team to coach?" I hadn't paused to think about the specifics of Koa leaving town. Just always assumed he'd go, like before. Only…now it seems less appealing to have him leave. And this worries me. I don't have it in me to miss someone. I feel myself starting to need Koa, and I know damn well that needing someone inevitably results in them leaving me wanting.

I pull myself up from Koa's lap and look into his eyes.

"I'll always find a team to coach, Love. That's no bother. What's wrong?"

I shake my head and take a step backward, only to have him tug me closer. "Watch it, Esther. You'll get run over." I hear a whoosh as another woman runs past, only to be tackled into the sand by the opposition. It looks dreadfully painful, but everyone gets to their feet and keeps on running. It reminds me of herding my sisters down the street when we'd get evicted, each of us hauling a black trash bag full of whatever wouldn't split the seams. Just keep on going, no matter what knocked us down.

"I need some water," I croak, and then I shake away his hand as I head to the boardwalk in search of concessions.

30

KOA

Esther's gone long enough that I have to focus on my next match before she returns to the team canopy. The second match is a lot tougher than the first, and I'm pretty beat up by halftime, but something about seeing her on the sidelines sipping lemonade gives me an energy boost.

She's like a good luck charm, with her cheeks pinched in concern. Growing up in New Zealand, everyone played rugby, and both my parents knew enough about the game that they didn't worry I'd be killed in every friendly match. Playing here in the States, all the mums wince and the players' girlfriends cringe. Not that Esther is my girlfriend. I can't imagine using the word girl to describe her, even in her youth.

Something tells me she's been an old soul her entire life.

At any rate, it revs my engine knowing she cares what happens to me, so I barely stop when a big fella plows me out of bounds the second I catch a wild pass from our halfback. Esther nearly drops her lemonade rushing over to check on me, but I'm back on the pitch and chasing the ball in a flash. I give her a wink when I'm able.

After the match, she's quiet while we all laze about in the shade. I run a hand up her calf as she stands above me. "That game was a lot different than the first one." She frowns.

"Tougher competition, isn't it? The next one will be harder yet, since we'll play another team who has won two."

"How many games will you play today?" She crosses her arms and glances at the ocean.

I shrug. "I can stop any time, Love. Truly. But just the one more, if you're asking."

She sighs and sits down in the sand. "Aren't you hungry? I'm hungry and I was just watching."

"I'm always hungry, Esther. You going to make me a sandwich, then? I see you're already barefoot."

Her face turns the color of a tomato, and she tackles me harder than that bloke from the second match. I wince as her elbow digs into my shoulder. I must have a tender spot. Esther sees and frowns. "Did I hurt you? Or was that from the game?"

"A little of both, I reckon." I massage the area, which hurts worse from the sand stuck to my sweaty hands. "I should take a dip. Ice baths are good for recovery."

Dozer laughs and shakes his head. "You're nuts, man. I saw the water is 67 degrees today."

I ignore the lads and tug on Esther's hand. "You fancy a frigid dip?"

Esther opens her mouth to say something, probably of the horrified variety, but her phone starts ringing loudly. I frown. "I thought you were turning that off?" She cringes and fumbles to silence it, but I don't miss her glancing at the screen. "I wish your sisters would let you have a day off. Just one."

Esther manages to silence the phone and looks at me icily. "Today is the second day, actually. And that was Chloe calling."

"Well, your friends should definitely let you have a day off. What could she possibly need from you when she knows you're with me?"

Esther crosses her arms and the rugby guys back away, in search of sustenance. "Sometimes friends call each other to hear how things are going, Koa. Maybe she wants to know —" Esther bites her lip and holds up her hand. "I don't know why I snap at you. What does it matter? I have responsibilities, as I've said. I'm sorry the phone rang. I did, in fact, watch you play rugby. Twice." She hugs her arms against herself more tightly. I climb to my feet and sigh.

"Look, I'm sorry I snapped about the phone." I drag a hand through my hair, feel how sweaty it is, and wipe my palm on my shorts. "I just wish the people in your life would give you this much space." I hold up a thumb and forefinger, nudging it closer and closer to her until she laughs and untangles her arms. "I want you to be able to relax if you're forced to go on this awful trip with me and all."

I nudge her, teasing. It works. She smiles faintly. "It's been a nice trip."

I grin. "It'll be nicer once you've gone in the ocean. Come onnnnn, live a little." I take the phone from her and toss it on my chair along with my shirt. She runs her tongue over her lips and boldly, I reach for the hem of her t-shirt. "Come in the sea with me and help me ice my shoulder."

"You're nuts, you know that?" Her words have no heat behind them, and she tugs the shirt over her head, revealing the bikini I caught sight of when she first opened her bag at the hotel. I whistle out a slow breath, eyeing every inch of her soft skin on display. She's round and lush, her breasts ripe and spilling from the triangle top of the suit. "Christ, Esther."

"Christ, Koa!" She shrieks in the water, bobbing to the surface, teeth chattering. We held hands and ran for it, knees churning through the waves until we were in up to our shoulders. "I can't feel my feet. Seriously, I'm getting hypothermia."

"Come here, then." I pull her into my arms, feeling her toes against my legs as she wraps her body fully around me. The rocking motion of the icy waves drives us closer together, and I squeeze my treat tighter.

"Does this hurt your shoulder?" She peers at the appendage with concern on her face in between shivers.

"What shoulder?" I squeeze her ass, feeling her chilled, slippery skin under the water. I grow hard despite my frozen balls. She notices and stills. Her expression softens.

I'm suddenly longing for home, even as I realize I'm not sure what that means. So I tell Esther, "We have a tradition back home. The Māori people do, I mean."

"Tell me about it." Esther smiles and shivers a bit. I hug her closer.

"It's a greeting, but I think we can still do it if you're game." My palms press into her hips. She nods. "It's called hongi. We press our foreheads together and our noses."

"We're basically doing that already." Her teeth are really chattering now.

"Close your eyes and breathe with me, through your nose." We do, and between the smell of the sea and the feel of Esther, it's like I'm home. I remember pressing noses with my long-gone grandparents. I remember doing it with my parents, too. I don't feel a longing, I feel anchored.

"We've shared breath," I tell her, and she nods.

"That was really nice."

"Yeah. It is nice. Maybe a little less when you do it with a crusty old bloke. Heh."

"Koa."

"Yes, Love?"

"I need to get out of this water."

I nod my head and start to walk toward the shore, making her laugh some more until a wave crashes over the both of us, and she starts coughing up sea water. "Let's get you warm, pet."

"Don't call me that."

"Why?"

I wrap a towel around her and rub her dry as she stares at me with those huge eyes of hers. "It feels weird."

"As you wish, then."

"Hey, Koa, you in for the next match, man? We just heard from Chaz, and he'll actually be here in time..." Dozer appears over Esther's shoulder, looking sheepish.

I don't take my eyes off Esther, and I don't stop rubbing her dry with the towel. "Perfect, mate. I'll sit this one out. Where's the social, then?"

"Oh, thanks, man. Right here! Bonfire and pig roast right on the beach. You and your lady in? We've got extra tickets." He roots around in his bag and procures two fluorescent bookmarks.

"See you then, Doze." He and the lads head down the beach for the final game. I stoop to gather our things and tip a chin toward our hotel. "Come on, Esther. Let's get you in the hot tub."

31

ESTHER

I don't know why I keep pecking at Koa for saying random shit. I find myself snapping at him like I do my sisters, only instead of telling me he's sorry, he snaps right back at me. It's unnerving.

And yet, I let him lead me by the hand through the hotel lobby, hardly worrying that I'm in a bikini wrapped in a too-small towel as he wanders around wearing only swim trunks, confident as a peacock. The man struts. "You're strutting," I mutter.

"Damn right. Look at you." He jabs a thumb at the elevator and starts rubbing my arms. "Who wouldn't strut with you on their arm?"

I've always been pretty confident about my body. I know people lust after me. But there's something about this man's gaze, about the confidence and surety he shows in his lust for me...it makes me feel exposed.

Once we're in the elevator, he boxes me against the wall, and I feel his cool breath on my forehead. He's so warm, always, despite the frigid ocean. I had no idea it would feel and taste that way. I'm not sure I liked feeling it, although

Koa promises it's better when it's warm. Better in New Zealand.

"It takes a very special woman to give me wood in a frozen ocean, Esther. A very special woman indeed."

I glance down at his crotch and see he is once again bulging out of his shorts. I bite my lip, but the elevator slides open for the rooftop pool. There's nobody up here at all, just the blue rectangle of heated pool and, over in one corner, the steaming hot tub with frothing water. "Oh, that looks nice." I drop the towel on the deck, forgetting about the handsome Māori man in my arms, and I make a beeline for the hot water.

"Oh god," I groan as I sink into the foam. "This *is* so nice."

Koa makes a move like he's going to jump in, and I shriek. "No, Koa, don't, you'll hurt yourself." But then he winks and steps one long leg into the middle of the tub. And he winks. Again. What must it feel like to so confidently know nothing bad will happen?

And then I remember that bad things have, in fact, happened to Koa. He was yanked from his home as a kid and then lost the only family he had on this earth. He's alone, and despite all that, he lives joyfully. Like he doesn't have a care in the world.

He pulls me onto his lap, and I let him. Then I revel in the feel of his lips on my neck. "You're so firm...and your lips are so soft." I feel drunk in the heat after the shock of the cold ocean.

"Oh, I'm firm, Hun." He thrusts up against me, and I almost laugh. I almost push him away. But I don't. I wriggle my hips and bask in the contented moan this draws from his throat.

"Yes, I can feel that." I lean in and nip at his jaw, letting my nipples drag against his chest through the material. When I first put on the bikini, I was cursing my friends for meddling, for packing such an indecent and insufficient bathing suit. But when I saw the look in Koa's eye as he stared at me, I changed my mind about all of it.

"Esther," he breathes into my ear. He looks around the rooftop. "I don't want to mess up the hot tub. But I very much want to mess up the hot tub."

"It's a real problem," I agree, grinding against him again in the warm, slick water. With a deep sigh and a lot of conviction, I ease myself from his lap and climb out of the tub. I grab two of the towels on the pool deck and wrap them both around myself as Koa watches from the hot tub, his hands clasped behind his head, his grin lascivious and wicked. "Are you coming or what?"

WE DESTROY THE HOTEL ROOM. He heaves me onto the table at first, and I wrap my legs around his body while he bites my bikini off and hurls it on the floor with a wet slap. We make out for a while until I slither out from under him and then trip on the carpet. He dives on top of me on the floor and sucks on my nipples as I use my feet to inch his wet trunks down his hips.

Naked, we pant and grind against one another. Our hands are everywhere, our moans are deafening. "Condom," he groans out, easing himself from on top of me with obvious effort. I shove him back on the bed and kneel between his massive thighs. I toss my wet hair over one shoulder and gaze up at him. I know I have all the power in the world right now.

I grasp his cock at the root, my fist rubbing against the

course, scant hair there. "You're so smooth," I murmur as I give him a stroke. He nods and reaches for my hair. I lick my lips and then lick the brown tip of him. He shudders in my hands, and I kiss his length.

"Esther." His voice is so reverent. I'm so overwhelmed by his vulnerability, by the way he trusts me with his most delicate bits. I wrap my lips around his length, feeling him slide into my mouth. I moan as I let the tip of him hit the back of my throat and ease off. He emits low, keening sounds as I make myself comfortable.

Koa surrenders to me, leaning back on the bed, never taking his eyes off me as I begin to bob my head up and down on his cock. I don't like giving head, as a rule. But it feels like a boss move with Koa, even knowing he's sweaty and covered in ocean and hot tub. I have him totally at my mercy right now, and I fucking love this. I adjust my weight, settling lower on my knees and Koa whimpers as I clutch his thighs in each hand, letting my head maneuver without assistance. He's so hard, it's easy to navigate. I feel him swell in my mouth, and I pull off with a wet pop. I glance up at him, at those dark reverent eyes, and I back away, toward the shower.

32

KOA

I am unprepared for how it feels to need Esther's touch like this. I crave her, not because she is new and willing, but because she is familiar and exquisite. She just knelt before me to give me pleasure in a way I would never have imagined, and now she's tempting me to follow her into the shower.

I cannot resist. I step into the steamy, warm oasis with this woman and all her curves, and all her dark hair, and I fold my body around all of it. My mouth seeks her skin, conveying what I can't bring myself to say out loud.

We bicker and pick at one another, and we don't yet understand each other's motivations, but I need her. This is startlingly clear to me in this moment. I need Esther Storm, and that terrifies me. But more than my fear, I feel an overpowering throb of happiness because I know she needs me, too, damn it.

We need each other.

"Koa." My name on her lips is like magic to me, and I look into her dark eyes as they try to focus. "Koa, I need you." She rocks her hips against me, straddling my thigh and seeking release. She needs me for that, but I know she needs me for everything we've been doing since I came back into town. She needs me to remind her that she's more than the oldest sister. She's more than a badass bartender and business owner.

She's somebody's everything. I reach between her legs, my thumb pressing where I know she needs my touch. It doesn't take long. I'm not sure if it's the way she made herself vulnerable, or if it really did turn her on to take my cock in her mouth, but in a matter of moments, Esther is groaning my name, wriggling against my hand, riding my thigh.

I grunt and spin her around in my arms, holding her tight against my chest as I continue to rub her clit with one hand and allow my other to enjoy the wonder of her chest. God, I love Esther's boobs. And then I remember how much I love her ass, so I release her in order to take hold of that backside with both my hands. She braces herself against the shower wall and looks over her shoulder at me.

"I'm on birth control," she pants. "I want you inside me." She bites her lip, still breathing heavy. "Right now, Koa."

She doesn't have to ask me twice. Guided by some sort of divine assistance, I plunge inside her heat in one thrust. She is so soft, so pliant. We both grunt as we collide. I know it won't be long, between the steam and the sight of her covered in water, the memory of her mouth around my shaft. "Esther," I breathe. "Love."

She braces her hands against the tile and begins to thrust back against me. The feel of her, slick, bare, and so tight against my cock, is like nothing I've ever experienced. I'm gone to the sensation, tumbling with her in a giant wave, spending myself inside her as she comes in my arms. I am suddenly desperate to hold her, facing me, and I pull out and spin her right back around. I ease my mouth against hers, moaning softly into the kiss. Have we kissed like this? Softly, slowly, tenderly? I lean back against the tile, needing the support as I sink into the emotions of what we've done.

Esther rests her cheek against my chest and lets me hold her. I feel her allow me inside. I feel our heartbeats begin to sync. I know in this moment that I cannot let her go. Not after our interview with immigration. Not after the trip back to Pittsburgh. I'm not leaving this woman.

ESTHER IS quiet as we dress for the barbecue. I assure her a rugby party on the beach does not require any special care in terms of outfit, but apparently her friends have invaded her suitcase, filling it with lacy underthings and sexy dresses.

She holds up two outfits that would be great for a society wedding and gestures between them. "Which one will be less awful if I get sauce on it while I eat?"

I point to the blue one, not because I think it's a better fit for barbecue sauce but because I can't wait to see her wearing it. "You'll look amazing in this one."

"Who will see me? It's dark."

"I'll see you. And I'll know." I nod and sit on the bed, already wearing khaki shorts and a polo. I watch shamelessly as my wife gets herself ready. I love that I'm the only one who gets to see her this way, unkempt, as she prepares her armor before heading into the world.

"It looks so nice with your skin. How do you manage to stay so pale, by the way? Do you never go outside."

She shrugs. "I live in Pittsburgh. We have less sun than Seattle. Or so I've heard."

Esther leans toward the mirror and applies bright red lipstick, pressing her lips together a few times to make sure the color coats each inch of those plump pillows. I look away before my thoughts send us right back into the shower.

I hear her phone buzzing on the nightstand, and I growl at it. "I'm going to turn this off." I reach for it, but she whips her head around.

"Please don't. The bar should be in full swing right now. I just...I need Eva to be able to reach me. I'm sure the messages are just the Foof gals bantering about someone's pregnancy or someone else's corporate takeover."

I glance at the message previews. I see a few notes from Samantha and nod, swiping to clear the notifications.

We walk across the street to the beach, and it's not hard to spot the bonfire from the rugby tournament. From the sound of things, a lot of people have been using cheap beer to re-hydrate after a day running around in the sun. "Do you want food or a drink first?"

I suspect I know the answer, and Esther clutches at her stomach, the growling audible over the music and howling from the athletes. "I was promised pig roast."

I squeeze her hand, and we head to the food table where the line is considerably shorter than the line for the keg. "Let's sit," she says, after filling her plate. "We can get a drink later."

"Fair enough. Or someone might bring us one if they see us with empty hands." I find a log that's not yet been burnt, and Esther and I squeeze ourselves onto it. I hardly mind that only one cheek fits, pressed as I am against her with our food balanced on our knees.

Esther chews and looks to our right, where a group of women are shouting and gesturing wildly. "Did they just say something about a professional rugby team?" Esther looks back to me. "I didn't think we had that in this country."

I fork a bite of mashed potatoes which shouldn't be beach food, but really hits the spot right now. "I heard something about that, yeah. A few cities have pilot programs to see if they can drum up interest from fans." I swallow my mouthful. "Ever since the last Olympics there's been some talks."

Dozer spots us and makes his way through the throng, grinning. "Koa, mate, thanks again for helping us out today. What a win."

"No problem," I tell him, meaning it. "It was good to see you and the lads again."

Esther points her fork at the conversing women. "Did they say Pittsburgh? For the pro rugby thing?"

Dozer nods. "Yeah, man, we might be in sooner than you think to get that drink you promised us. Pittsburgh's holding an open tryout for men and women." I feel Esther's phone vibrate in the pocket of her dress, pressed against my own leg. I frown at it, but she glances up at Dozer, delighted.

"I never stopped to think it'd be women, too. Professional rugby for women! I can't wait to tell my friend Chloe. She's a soccer player."

"Well, you can wait at least one day," I snap, regretting my tone, but Esther doesn't notice. She finishes her food and pulls herself up to her feet. "Dozer, introduce me to those women. They said they'd come to try out."

I shovel a last bite of food in my mouth and hurry to follow D and Esther. By the time I join the conversation, she's inviting them to her bar, offering them the use of her sisters' bedrooms while they're in town to try out, and seemingly in awe of their status as almost-professional athletes. I try to rein in my jealousy, but I do not succeed. Esther is mine, damn it. I don't want to share her. Not with house-guests, not with anyone.

"Koa, this is Annie and Kayleigh. We saw them play earlier today."

"Koa Stewart." I hold out a hand, and the one called Annie gives me a shake. She smiles.

"We met you in Boulder, I think. Or maybe Nashville. One of those. You were coaching an all-star team."

Kayleigh nods vigorously. "Yeah! That's right. Any thoughts on our loss today? I really thought we had that team from Albany..."

Esther stares at me intently as I ask them questions about how they planned for the match, why *they* think things fell apart. I start to hope Esther's interest means she wants me around, that she's dreaming about a rugby community in Pittsburgh that lets me stay near her.

Or maybe I'm the one hoping for that?

Annie asks me for workout tips for the month remaining before the tryout, but I'm distracted by Esther's phone which she pulls out of her pocket. How can I dream about a lifetime with this woman when she can't even give me an evening? The people in Esther's life aren't going anywhere. She frowns at the screen, and I snap.

"One night, Esther. Come on." I snatch the phone from her and power it off, stuffing it into my own pocket as she glares at me. Annie and Kayleigh grimace.

Kayleigh pats Annie's arm. "We'll catch up with you later..."

They disappear into the dark as Esther boils.

"What the fuck, Koa? You had no right. That could have been important." Esther is seething, reaching around me, and trying to get her phone back. I feel petty and childish, but I'm also irate that her social network couldn't make a temporary Esther-free group chat for a few damn days.

And then my phone starts ringing. Persistently.

Esther yanks it from my hand and stares at the screen. "It's AJ." She fumbles around and tries to unlock the device.

"Here, let me—"

"I've got it. AJ. Hello? What's wrong?"

A few beats later, Esther screams.

33

ESTHER

Fire.

AJ said there was a fire. I hear and feel myself screaming as I wade through the sand, trying to get to the boardwalk, to the hotel.

"Can you tell me again?"

His voice is so calm, as if he's not delivering news of a disaster. "Esther, your sisters are all fine. Nobody was injured. Everyone is safe."

I freeze. Why hadn't I considered people? My first thought was the bar. Why are my priorities so broken?

I sink to the ground. "Is Eva there?"

"Yes. All your sisters are here, and so are Sam and Chloe and Piper. They've all been at the bar both nights, just to support Eva if she needed a hand."

"They were?" Relief washes over me, knowing all my sisters are safe. Just as quickly, the panic sets back in as I worry about the bar. I sense a presence next to me, and I don't have the spare energy to see if it's a stranger or if it's Koa. I hope it's Koa. Whoever it is sits next to me and wraps an arm around my shoulders.

"People have been trying to reach you for some time, Esther. I'm so sorry. I know this trip is important to you. Samantha remembered that I have Koa's number, and she asked me to call."

I stare up to my right, where Koa's face is etched in concern under the streetlight. My throat is full of sand. My stomach heaves. I knew something like this would happen. I sensed it.

You don't grow up bouncing from one shitty apartment to another with a trash bag over one shoulder and then casually take vacations like nothing will happen. Something always happens.

"Esther, I'm handing the phone to Sam, okay?" I hear a shuffling sound and then my friend's voice.

"Esther, first of all, it's going to be all right. I promise. You have insurance, right?"

"Insurance?" I feel frantic and stand again, pacing as I slap Koa's arm away when he tries to hug me. "I have no idea where the policy info is. I mean, it should be in the office. Did the office burn down? Oh my god. Did anything burn down?"

"Esther!" Sam's voice is sharp, authoritative. "Listen, sweetie. Nothing burned down. The fire started back in the alley. Your neighbors tossed paint thinner in the trash bins. It was hot as Hades here today, and it caught on fire."

"Okay." I fight my urge to repeat my questions about the office. Why can't Samantha parse all this down to the crucial bits of information I'd already know if I was there, where I belong?

"The sprinklers went off, so there's some water damage inside. And smoke smells. The firefighters had, like, a packet of what to do. They gave it to Eva."

"I need to come back."

"There is nothing you can do tonight other than call your insurance. They won't send anyone until morning. The building next door wasn't as lucky, so the fire guys are still over there."

"Where are you? Where are my sisters?"

Sam laughs. "We're standing on Butler Street along with half of Lawrenceville, rubbernecking and staring at the firefighters. Hey, Lyra, do we do any research support for firefighters?" I hear a muffled sound in the background before Samantha returns to the call. "There's a lady firefighter here, too. Everyone is so sexy, Esther. Chloe, are you taking pictures? Okay, good."

"Sam! I'm coming back."

Koa stands in my path at those words. His jaw is clenched. His eyes intense.

Sam hums. "Esther, like I said you can't do anything tonight."

"I'm six hours away. It'll take me until almost business hours to get back anyway."

"Esther, I really think you should—"

I gasp as Koa snatches the phone from my hand. "Samantha? Hey, Hun, it's Koa. Esther and I are going to talk things over, and she will communicate the plan from her phone in a bit, yeah?" He pinches his lips together. "Right. Until then."

"What the fuck, Koa? Come on. We have to get our stuff and hit the road."

He puts a meaty paw on my shoulder. "Esther, we have our interview in the morning."

I stare at him. "You can't possibly think I'm going to be able to do that right now, Koa."

"Esther, it's been put off for five years. This is the federal government. We can't just reschedule. You realize what will happen if we skip this, right?"

I start crossing the street toward the hotel, shaking my head as I shout. "This is a fucking emergency, Koa. My business caught on fire. I'm sure they will understand."

"And I'm sure they will not. Esther, you heard Samantha. Nobody was injured. The bar suffered only mild damage."

"Nobody said the word mild. Where are you getting mild?"

I realize I sound like a maniac, but I certainly can't find my Zen, and he's not helping. At all.

"Esther, some water damage and some smoke smells. I promise you, insurance can handle this without you being there. I'm asking you to calm down and—"

"Do. Not." I shove him against the wall in the lobby. "Tell. Me. To calm down. Never tell me to calm down!" I realize I'm shouting and shoving him, and he's big and barely moves under my pushes. The elevator arrives. I'm sure people are staring at us because Koa places a gentle hand on my back and guides me into the elevator.

"I'm asking you, please, to take a breath. Let's sit down and drink some water and make a plan."

"I have a plan, Koa. My plan is to get into *my* car and drive back to Pittsburgh to *my* bar and *my* family." I stalk out of the elevator and fish around for our room key, remembering that Koa keyed everything into our phones. And he still has mine. I cross my arms over my chest and tap a toe as I wait for him to open the door, and then I immediately begin shoving my things back into my bag.

"I'm not going to let you drive in this condition, Esther. You aren't making safe choices right now."

I grind my teeth together, enraged at his audacity. "Give me my keys. Give them to me now."

"I will not do that." He crosses his arms over his chest. "We have an agreement, you and me. Are you going to break it now? Leave me hanging at the last second?"

I scream, not a shriek but a deep, primal growl from way inside my chest. I never asked for an additional responsibility, another person to rely on me. I shove him and this time he stumbles back toward the bed. "Why do you want this so much, Koa? Why not go back to New Zealand and see your precious ocean? What is even here for you?"

I'm crying now, thinking of all the times I wished I could just escape, wished I had somewhere else to go, another life to lead that didn't include so many sisters with so much lice. And here is this man with all the money in the world and the opportunity to just fuck off into the sunset.

He grips the comforter and stares at me, looking wounded. "Everything, Esther. Everything is here, and I hate that you can't see that."

34

KOA

Esther wakes with the sun and silently packs her bag. I follow suit and check out. I assume she's prepared to go ahead with our plan, to play the part during our interview. She doesn't look like a blushing bride, however. She says nothing, just stares out the window as I drive to Philadelphia and park in the garage near the immigration offices.

I thought the building's interior would be glowing white, like the hospital hall where I went to identify my parents. I actually feel the same level of dread. Like I have a marble in my windpipe and a sea of snakes in my belly. Like nothing will ever be right again.

This place is depressing. Everything is brown or tan, and while I know it's been decades since anyone could smoke inside, I think I catch a whiff of cigarettes at every turn.

Esther's like a ghost beside me, emanating fumes of worry and frustration. She was up all night on the phone with Eva and Samantha. I heard her begging them for details of the fire, arguing until her voice was hoarse when the ladies in Pittsburgh wouldn't cross the fire department barricades. I'm glad I didn't let her drive then, because she wasn't making rational choices. I know Esther wants to be in Pittsburgh fretting over her bar, but damn it, this is the entire reason she has the bar. This interview, this moment—this is everything. I don't know what happens to Esther if this goes to shit...but I know I'll be wondering it from another hemisphere. I can't be a stranger in an unfamiliar place again. I can't let that happen.

I check in at the desk, and sit next to my wife, who tolerates my presence but stiffens when I place a hand on her leg. I barely had time to admire her in the dress her friends must have shoved in the bag. I notice she didn't wear the same one she had on last night at the barbecue. Probably because she got sand and tears all over it when she found out about the fire.

I sigh and try to adjust myself in the seat. It's a tight fit with the arms of the chair pinching into my torso. They never seem to make furniture with bulky blokes in mind.

Soon enough, we're called back and seated opposite a man in a cheap suit, cheap glasses, and a cheaper haircut.

"Right. Mr. and Mrs. Stewart. Pleased to meet you at last."

I clear my throat. "My wife kept her maiden name. She's Ms. Storm, if you please."

The man frowns and looks at his folder, making a note. "Right. Well, I'm Mr. Reese, and we have just a few questions before we can proceed with your green card application." He clicks a pen. "Mind telling me how you met?"

I launch into our practiced story, waiting for Esther to chime in with her typical punchy quips about being mean to me from the get-go, but me finding that irresistible. But she's silent, her lip occasionally trembling.

Mr. Reese looks concerned. "Ms. Storm, is that accurate? You served Koa drinks at a bar where you worked?"

She nods her head, lip wobbling some more.

I swallow and lean forward. "My wife had some unfortunate news last night. A fire at her business. She's anxious to get back to Pittsburgh and see to the aftermath."

Mr. Reese frowns. "That's odd timing. Ms. Storm, has there ever been this type of incident before? A fire on the premises?"

Her eyes flare, and she drops her jaw. "No," she says, her voice full of ire. "Of course not."

Reese adjusts his tie. "Well, I won't keep you longer than necessary. Mr. Stewart, I notice that you travel quite a lot. Can you explain this? It seems your wife does not accompany you."

Esther snorts. I glare at her. "My work as a rugby coach takes me all over. Absence makes the heart grow fonder, right?"

"Hmm." Reese makes abrupt notes in the file. "By my estimates you've spent very little time in Pittsburgh since your marriage, Mr. Stewart. Quite the roster of coaching positions..."

I run a hand along the back of my neck, trying to remember the phrasing we thought up for this line of questioning. "I have a unique skill set, being Kiwi. Rugby is in my blood. A lot of teams here are eager to pay for that expertise."

Reese frowns. "So, you're saying you have financial motivations?"

Esther slaps the desk, and we all jump. "Doesn't everyone work for pay? Of course, he's motivated by money."

I can't help the grin that tips my lips upward as Esther

defends me, despite her deep anger at being here. I think of everything we've been through the past few weeks...hell, the past five years. I realize I don't want to be deported because I don't want to be away from this woman. I need her. I need her very badly.

And she needs me. Suddenly, I'm motivated to convince her just how much she needs me. We are meant for one another, whether she likes it or not.

Mr. Reese squints and, again, jots notes in his folder. He keeps the whole thing angled toward him, so we can't peek. I sense it's not going well. I pull out my phone. "Care to take a look at some pictures of us at the beach? We were told to prepare some mementos—"

"I'm sure the time stamps for those will be fairly recent." Reese sniffs and then sits back in his chair. He looks between us. "Look, I can tell you two can barely stand one another. I don't think there's any sense in continuing this ruse."

"You're wrong." I sit back in my own chair. "I'm mad for this woman. Ask me anything. Ask me why I taught her sister to fry an egg or went grocery shopping with her friends' boyfriends. Ask me why I peeled labels off Jesus candles. Ask me what she looks like asleep at dawn, with the sunrise glinting off the tips of her lashes. But don't you tell me I can't stand her."

Esther turns to me, and she has tears welling in her eyes. She shakes her head. "Koa," she whispers. "Don't."

I lick my lips and keep my eyes on Esther as I tell Reese my final secret. "And I know my wife looks salty at the moment—who wouldn't if their establishment caught fire? But I can tell you she's as sentimental as she is crabby. She's still got the flower I gave her at our wedding, pressed and dried in her bedroom along with every postcard I ever sent her."

The tears in Esther's eyes spill over at this last revelation, at the results of my snooping.

Esther closes her eyes and takes a few deep breaths. "I can't do this anymore." It's unclear if she's talking to me or to Reese or to us both. "I have to go."

She takes off the hall at a jog, and I chase after her, knowing I'm blowing my only chance to remain here. Knowing that now, I might leave this country in handcuffs, but not wanting to let Esther go in this state of upset.

I find her on the corner, trying to hail a taxi. "Esther, wait. Please."

"I'm going to the airport, Koa. Do whatever you want with my car." I run toward her, wanting to explain that I can get her to Pittsburgh just as fast as she can deal with security and catch a ride home from the Pittsburgh airport. But she's jumping into a yellow car and slamming the door in my face before I can reach her.

35

ESTHER

> I'm on a plane home. Can you get me at the airport in an hour?

EVA

I don't have a car...

I groan, remembering that Koa has my car somewhere in downtown Philadelphia.

EVA

Before you ask, the timing just really, really sucks, Esther. The others all took time off to help me at the bar, and they all have to work.

EVA

Eliza has the truck out with the goats, Eden drove to New York to buy a queen or something, and Eila also doesn't have a car. I'm so sorry.

EVA

You're gonna have to take the bus, sis.

Like hell I will. I've never actually asked Foof for help

before, but I'm in enough of a panic that I fire off an S.O.S. before the flight attendant burns me with the sparks shooting out of her eyes as the plane taxis on the runway.

I paid way too much money for this last-minute flight, but my bones are literally screaming at me to get back to my bar. A fucking fire. A fire!

Of all the things I've seen and done in my life, fire has been the least expected. Which is dumb because my mom brought a lot of men into our hovels smoking cigarettes and passing out on couches with them lit. I should have been worried about fire for years.

I stare out the window, wondering how fire escaped my subconscious as a worry topic, and almost as soon as we hit cruising altitude, the captain announces that we've begun our descent into Pittsburgh. The second the wheels hit the ground, I turn my phone back on and exhale.

The barrage of messages feels like a warm hug.

SAM

Lyra, tell the new clients I'm sorry and I have to reschedule. Esther, I got you.

CHLOE

Sam, let me grab Esther. My schedule is more flexible.

PIPER

I don't have clients until 2. I can also get Esther.

LYRA

Have asked admin team to reschedule with new client. Sam, want to ride together to Bridges and Bitters?

SAM

Okay, okay, Chloe called dibs. See you all in Lawrenceville?

PIPER

I will bring meatballs.

CHLOE

That is an excellent plan.

I don't have any luggage, which is probably why I got a cavity search at security in Philadelphia, but it also means I can sprint to the land-side terminal the second I get off the plane.

Chloe waves at me, and I leap in the car. "Go, Chloe. Floor it."

She shakes her head at me. "Esther, you know my EV isn't zippy. We're going to go at a reasonable speed, though, and I promise everything will be okay."

I don't look at her, and I don't feel capable of responding. How on earth could anything be okay, ever again? I said terrible things to Koa, I probably cost him his ability to stay in this country, my fucking business is destroyed.

And then I imagine Koa leaving, never being allowed to return. I broke all my goddamned rules, and now he's going to have to leave, and it will be my fault. I can't fix this. I can't fix the bar. I only have the bar because of him. I'm so messed up right now that I imagine I can feel him near me, imagine I can hear his voice.

I can barely breathe.

I rub a knuckle along my sternum. Chloe frowns. "You're not having actual chest pains, are you? Do we need to go to Mercy hospital?"

I shake my head. "It's just stress. I'll breathe easy when I see it. I think. I hope. Did you see it?"

I hear my voice crack with that last question and Chloe sighs. "I was there. We were all there. But the firefighters wouldn't let us back inside last night, so I don't really know the aftermath. I think it's all just wet and smelly, though. Not awful..."

I unclench a tiny bit when I see there's no traffic at the tunnel, and Chloe zips across the bridge. I grip the armrest silently until she eases into a parking spot across from the bar.

I sprint across the street and rip down the yellow caution tape slung across the door, cursing when I realize it's been left unlocked overnight.

But once I get inside, I see that no thief in their right mind would view this place as a target right now.

It looks like one of those pictures people post of buildings where nature has taken back over. There aren't plants growing out of my floor, but the dripping wallpaper and light fixtures, the charred walls...it all looks surreal and post-apocalyptic.

My carefully curated bench seats are sooty. The barstools are tipped over and chipped from where people evidently fled in haste. The liquor bottles are smashed, and flies swarm around a bowl of citrus.

The flies are what get me.

I sink to the floor and sob.

AN UNDETERMINED AMOUNT of time later, I feel warmth around me. I open my eyes to see my friends kneeling on the ground with their hands on my back. Nobody speaks. They're just there, eyes glittering with their own tears. Seeing them upset snaps me out of my misery, and I spring to my feet.

"We have to get cleaning." I stalk behind the bar and find my stash of rags. Muttering to myself, I head down the reeking hall to the supply closet for the mop and bucket.

I realize nobody has followed me, but I fill the bucket with water and dump in extra Pine Sol. I can at least mop the floors. Or should I start with the walls? Start high and work down? I can mop walls, probably.

Back out in the main room, I fling bar towels at my friends. "We can do this. We can fix this."

I heave the mop from the bucket, wring it quickly, and slap it against a wall as high as I can reach. The mop pulls off more of the decorative paper. I give it a few shoves, and more of the same keeps happening. I'm making things worse.

I abandon the mop and start scrubbing the tabletops, watching in horror as I appear to be smearing the soot around rather than cleaning it up.

"Esther."

I hear someone calling my name, but I can't stop now. I have to scrape through this layer of grime. If I can clean one table, that'll be a place I can set things down, make lists. I can do this.

"Isn't anyone going to help me?"

I look over my shoulder and all my sisters are here. All my Foof friends are here. They're all standing around, watching me. None of them are lifting a finger.

"Come on! Help me!"

I return my gaze to the task at hand, using two hands on the rag, now black with grime and making not a lick of difference in the mess. I push as hard as I can, and nothing helps. I push again.

I start to moan in frustration, and I feel a hand on the small of my back. I swat at whoever it is. "If you're not going to help me, then get out!" I don't turn around as I furiously scrub at the table, starting to see a glimmer of the wood grain at last. Encouraged, I keep scrubbing.

I'm grunting with the effort now, making a small golden dent in the filth. My arms start to cramp, and I turn around, thinking to rinse the rag.

I see that my sisters have gone, my friends have gone. There's just one person standing between me and the mop bucket.

"How the hell did you get here?"

Koa sighs and steps toward me, arms wide.

36

KOA

Esther doesn't want me to hug her, but I do it anyway. She fights a bit, smacking me with the wet, dirty rag. But I've been wet and dirty before. I just spent five hours in a car speeding here to be with this woman because I can't bear to be without her, dirt be damned. I don't want her for her hygiene. I need her for the way she makes me feel like I belong. I hold my ground and wrap her in my arms and eventually, she lets go and sobs.

I pat her hair, not caring that it's grimy and we both smell like an ashtray at this point. "I told you I could drive about as fast as you could get a flight, pet."

"Not your pet."

"Chur." I smile into her hair. If she can have a go at me, then she's feeling a bit more in control. When I feel her breathing start to slow, I release my hug enough that she can lean back and make eye contact.

"Are you going to help me?"

"Of course I'm going to help you, Esther."

She sighs and wriggles out of my arms, tossing me a rag

from her heap. I catch it and shake my head. "This isn't the way, my love."

"What are you talking about? Start scrubbing. Did you see how I was making progress on this table?"

I look to the front of the bar and see a row of Storms and Foof friends with their faces pressed against the grimy glass, all needing to see if Esther will come through this crisis intact.

"Esther, come here." I reach for her, but she doesn't see or hear. She's scrubbing the table again with vigor, so I place my hands on her shoulders. "Esther. Where is your insurance information?"

"Office. Oh, that's a good idea, Koa. We need to get them to send a check."

"Esther. You cannot scrub this bar yourself."

"Of course I can. I am doing it right now."

I pull the rag from her hands, and she shrieks. I wrap her in my arms again, and I can feel a set of sobs brewing in her capable, competent chest. "Esther, Love, there are companies who do this. There are people with the right tools and the right chemicals. This is why you get insurance."

She shakes her head rapidly. "I have to fix this."

"It will be fixed. I promise."

More head shaking, so I pull her tighter against my chest. "There are professionals, who will look far less sexy than you bent over this table scrubbing. And we will call them, and they will fix your bar. It will be beautiful again, Love. I promise you. I promise it."

I can't think of the last time I promised someone anything. I know damn well that promising her this means sticking around for months, and I'm not even sure I can legally do that after this morning's fiasco. I didn't linger to hear the outcome. I told Reese I needed to see to my wife and sprinted out of the immigration building. They're probably sending people to deport me right now.

But I promise Esther all the same. And I don't feel anything other than determination to make it all come true. "I'm not going anywhere, Esther. And I'm going to help you, and what I mean by that is I'm going to help you call the right people to fix this."

Esther eventually lets go and just weeps. She snots and cries into my chest, and I feel relief. She drops the rag to the ground at last and digs her fingers into my back as she sobs. I lower us both to the floor.

A glance to the window shows me a row of women all fanning themselves in relief. It seems odd that such a large group of people should feel relief at seeing Esther fall to pieces, but I'm sure they share my realization that if she's letting things out, she feels safe enough with all of us to know we are here to pick it all up with her.

At one point, Samantha sneaks in and gestures that she's going down the hall to the office. She emerges with some papers and Esther's computer, and I see people outside going to town looking up files and making calls. "We've all got you, Esther," I whisper into her hair. "We love you."

A knot forms in my throat as I think about the implications of that. The last people I loved, the only people really, were my parents, and they fucking died.

The longer I hold my sobbing wife, wondering if I could possibly love her too, the sadder I feel. Soon, I'm crying right along with her. I didn't have time to cry after the accident. I had to deal with paperwork and finals week and worrying about getting deported. And then I graduated and had to deal with more paperwork, more concerns about getting deported. By the time I married Esther, I was used to shoving it all down, not thinking about anything.

So I sit here with my sobbing wife, and I sob alongside her. I sob for my parents. I sob for young Koa, dragged from New Zealand, never to see his mates again. I can't give that young man a hug or tell him everything will be all right. But I can grieve it all as part of my past even as I cling to the woman who will be my future. I'm better with her. Everything leading up to this helped me prepare for this fierce woman, and I'm not going anywhere. Never again.

I hear the front door creak open again, and someone clears their throat.

"Not a good time right now," I croak, without looking up.

The throat is cleared again, sharper now and with more intention. "I'm here from Immigration and Customs Enforcement," a deep voice announces. I stiffen. It didn't take them long to find us. Not long at all. "We've had a report of marriage fraud."

37

ESTHER

From the depths of my weeping, I hear a man saying I.C.E. has come for my husband. I freeze as I feel Koa stiffen around me.

I disentangle myself from his arms and look up at the man standing in the doorway, appearing like he wishes he was not standing in a fire hazard zone.

"Can't you see I need my husband right now?" I try to clear my hair from my face. I know I'm covered in soot and looking a mess. But also, who the hell does he think he is? First his organization shoves our paperwork to the side for five years, and now suddenly their lack of planning is our emergency? "As I mentioned in our interview this morning, we've had an emergency here in Pittsburgh."

I feel Koa's intake of breath as my tone gets bitchy with this officer. But that's how I roll. I don't let inspectors roll over my friends with nonsense bureaucracy, and I am not letting this man in weird trousers take my husband away from me.

I wave around the space, hoping he will tell his colleagues in Philadelphia that I wasn't kidding about the fire. "I think you can see that Koa and I are busy. I need his help. I need my husband."

I keep repeating this as I realize the truth of the words. I need him. I need Koa. I need someone to tell me when to stop doing everything my damn self. I need Koa to reassure me. And it doesn't feel terrible to need that, especially as he clutches me tighter the more I repeat my need for him. He's like a security blanket.

Or maybe this is just what it feels like to be secure?

I know my sisters love me. I feel that every second of every day. But they also depend on me. And I think I've created a similar relationship with my friends if I'm honest. I never let myself depend on anyone.

But I'm letting Koa hold me through this spewing of emotion, through this epic weakness. And...it's less terrifying. I really do feel like he will somehow help me make all of this okay.

If he's not deported.

The officer licks his lips and sniffs. "I can see there's been a fire. You did indicate an emergency in your interview this morning..." I nod rapidly. He scratches at his neck, like he's worried the soot in here will cling to his collar. It probably will. I'm probably going to get sick just from being inside this room with no mask.

"...bed check, but this is the address where you claim marital residence." I realize the officer has continued talking.

Koa looks at me. "You listed the bar as our address?"

I wince and nod.

He laughs. "Well, officer, it's mostly true. Some days we are here til all hours. But I'm working on getting her home more often."

Suddenly, Sam and Chloe and Piper burst in the front

door, waving a folder. "We talked to insurance. They're sending an adjuster right away, and they have, like, a whole list of companies who do this scrubbing. Esther, you can put down the mop!"

Piper looks at the immigration officer. "Are you from the insurance already?"

He shakes his head and opens his mouth to explain himself, but Sam cuts him off. "I got the insurance agent to give me an estimate, and Esther, they think you can be back open again in a few months. And the insurance will pay out whatever salary you would have earned during that time, including wages for your staff and ... who *is* this guy?"

Piper and Chloe look suspiciously at the immigration officer. I start to try and stand and talk to him in a way that's more dignified, but Koa keeps me locked in the circle of his arms. So, I stop fighting it. "He's from immigration," I choke out.

Piper scratches her chin. "I thought you met with them already. Ugh, Esther, I'm just so stinking sorry you had to end your beach trip early because of this fire situation. It just sucks so much!"

"Beach trip?" The immigration officer clicks his pen, like Piper just revealed some terrifying secret.

She nods her head and rattles on to him cheerfully. "Can you believe Esther never saw the ocean before this week? The ocean! Koa texted all the boyfriends this picture of her clapping her hands in the waves. How cute is she?"

Piper shows her phone to the officer, who nods at the image. "Oh, and here's this selfie. Or maybe someone else took it? Look at them canoodling on the beach! Aren't they so cute?"

I glance at Koa, who shrugs. "I thought you were so pissed that I was on my phone all the time?"

He grins. "I figured if I sent proof of life, they'd leave you alone."

As Piper tells the immigration officer all about Koa's use of the boyfriend group chat, I realize there's a method to her apparent vapid chatter. Slowly, cheerfully, she's explaining to him how Koa is woven into all of our lives. That he's not just an on-paper husband at all.

And the more she rattles on, explaining about him making guest appearances in her fitness classes and helping AJ with his grocery shopping, the more I realize it's all true.

Koa isn't an afterthought anymore. I can no longer imagine an existence where I only go home to sleep and clean, where I don't have someone making snarky remarks to me from the shower.

I don't want to return to that. I want him here. With me.

"I need you," I repeat, this time looking him in the eye.

He nods and kisses me on the forehead. When he pulls back, I can see soot on his lips. I suddenly want desperately to shower. "Koa, take me home. Please?"

38

KOA

I drive Esther home and start scouring her in the shower while Eva takes the car to get detailed. Each brush of the washcloth on her skin is a promise, from me to her. I will always show up for her. And it's okay for her to need that.

I keep hearing the echoes of her saying she needs me. And I need her, too. I kiss her forehead in the warm shower as she lets me take care of her, and I realize how much I need to take care of someone. This is what's been missing all this time.

I have time to mourn my parents. I have time to figure out my feelings about my home country. But right now, I have someone who needs me, and I have the ability to help her.

Along with all the other people who care about her, of course.

Samantha has set up operations in Esther's kitchen with Lyra there clacking furiously on her laptop, trying to integrate fire restoration research into their client base. Or something.

Eden hands me a shot glass full of honey and winks at me. "It's medicinal," she says. "It's a very hush-hush partnership I've got on the side." I arch a brow at her, and she rolls her eyes. "I put weed in the honey, Koa. To knock her out." Eden hooks a thumb at Esther, slumped on the floor in her shower.

"Ah," I toss a towel over my shoulder. "Good thinking." Eden smiles and blows Esther a kiss. Esther doesn't look up. "I'm going to tuck her into bed."

Eden nods. "That's for the best. Sam and Chloe said the insurance stuff is all handled. There's really nothing to do but wait and wait some more."

"Did Eva lock the door of the bar? I know Esther was worried about that."

"I will verify."

"Thanks, Eden." I don't stick around to watch her descend the steps. I head right back into the steam room Esther has created and open the glass door to the shower.

"Here you go, then, pet. Your sister made you something to help you sleep."

"Not your pet." Esther finally looks up at me and frowns. "You're going to get all wet."

"It's usually me saying that to you, isn't it?" I hold out the shot glass and Esther takes it. She looks up at me, confused, and I gesture for her to drink the golden elixir. It reminds me that I never got to eat Hokey Pokey with her on the beach.

There's a lot of things I never got to share with her. Or, rather, things we haven't *yet* gotten to share together. Because I'm not going anywhere. Piper saw to that. I grin, thinking of the folder of stamped paperwork on Esther's desk.

I hate that my wife is going through this setback with

her business, but I'm not going to lie. I'm relieved and pleased that I get to stick around and help her sort it.

"Can I wash your hair, Esther?" She nods, and I reach for the shampoo, rubbing it between my palms to make a lather.

I bury my fingers in her locks, loving the contrast of her black hair with my brown skin. "I love how we look together," I say above the sound of the water.

"We are both hella cute."

The funny honey must be setting in already because Esther giggles. "Let me help you stand." I heave her to her feet, and she slumps against me as I work my hands through her hair. I rinse the soap from her dark strands and massage her scalp. She keens, giving me all her weight.

"I think one more wipe with the loofa ought to do it," I tell her, and she doesn't react. I stretch to grab her scrubby and douse it with coconut body wash. I gently scrub every inch of her that I can reach while she's poured her weight on my shoulder. Then, I place her palms against the tile, and when I'm sure she's steady on her feet, I kneel before her in the shower, fully dressed, to scrub her legs and feet and belly.

Esther looks down at me, amazed, and doesn't speak.

All I can think is that it feels right to worship her like this, to take care of her. So I say, "I'll always be here for you, Esther. No matter what you need. Even if we disagree on what it is that you need."

That gets a smile from her, and I place a chaste kiss to her naval before shutting off the water. I reach out of the shower for the towels, wrapping her up tight before I quickly wipe off the worst of the running streams from my shorts.

"I'm going to tuck you into bed, Love. Do you need to use the toilet first?"

She takes care of business while I strip out of my sodden clothes. I wrap the towel around my waist and take Esther's hand as she stumbles into bed. "I'm so tired."

She closes her eyes, hair spread on the pillowcase. I know she didn't sleep well last night. I didn't either, worried about her, worried about her business, worried I did the wrong thing in asking her to wait 12 hours to keep our appointment.

We can discuss it all later, after she's had a proper rest. I tuck the covers under her chin and turn on the ceiling fan since I know she likes moving air while she sleeps. I smile when I see she's already poked her right foot out from the covers. Just the one foot.

I kiss her on the forehead and pull on a pair of shorts, heading downstairs to see what's to do.

The house is filled with people. Not just any people. Storm sisters, Foof women, and their partners. And from the smell of things, one of them brought food.

My stomach screams at me, a reminder I haven't eaten at all. Drawn by the smell, I head to the kitchen and groan at the sight of a taco bar.

Sam grins as I cram a ready-made taco into my mouth. She hands me a glass of water, which I chug before I can get to my manners. I see that Sam and Chloe and Piper are not just here for Esther...they're here for me, too. From the look on Samantha's face, I should have realized that a long time ago. Like when they put me in that group chat. "Cheers, Sam. Truly."

"Ah, don't worry about it. I forget to eat, too. AJ brought all this stuff."

I glance over at him, where he's poring over a spreadsheet with Lyra, talking about mold spores.

I figure I can thank him later, and I fix myself a plate and head to the dining room where there's a bit more space. I ease into a chair next to Chloe. She turns to me and smiles. "What a day, huh? Did I see you got your ... paperwork sorted out?"

"About time." I grunt as I down another taco in two bites, vowing to take my time with the third and eat like a civilized person.

Chloe's husband, Ted, nods and scratches at his chin. "So, what comes next then? Other than fire repair..."

Chloe laughs. "We all know Esther won't tolerate you working in her space."

I shrug because I truly don't know what I will do. My degree is in business administration, but all I've done for the past five years is drift around and coach.

Hearing my hesitation, Piper chips in with, "I was serious about you doing some guest teaching at Pipe Fitters. We do some family events where dads and kids come workout. You'd be great with those!"

"Cheers, Pipes. Appreciate it."

AJ drifts in from the kitchen with his own plate of tacos. He sits across from me and says, "You know, the public schools of Pittsburgh are always, always looking for coaches. And teachers."

"You have rugby in schools here?"

He shrugs. "Not yet..."

39

ESTHER

My entire house has been transformed. About a week after the fire, Koa got to work rearranging all the bedrooms on the second floor. Apparently, all my sisters encouraged this behavior. I wasn't even allowed to help, which was fine because I used all my nervous energy waterproofing the basement.

Eila's room is now full of workout equipment. Eden's room has two Murphy beds that fold down from the walls if guests want to sleep over. Eden insists she, Eila, and Eliza count as guests since they all have their own homes "like real-ass adults."

They tried to attribute that to me, but I told them to shut up. Eliza's room is a swanky office with a lot of computer monitors and video equipment Koa uses for his coaching.

Even though AJ wanted Koa to work for the public schools, Koa got an offer from that professional rugby league opening shop here in Pittsburgh. He's the director of the men's *and* women's teams, which means he will travel a lot.

I will never let anyone hear me say how much I miss him when he's on the road with the teams.

But I do miss him. I missed him when he took the teams for a weeklong tournament in Illinois. And now, three months later, I miss him even if he goes to a quick overnight in Ohio. Thankfully he distracts me with sex, so I don't dwell on feeling vulnerable.

"Esther, we've got a half hour." He shouts from the kitchen as I stare into the office adjacent to Eva's room. She still lives here, for now. She's also still working in the bar and convinced me to let her run point on the grand re-opening.

I head downstairs and accept the coffee my husband offers. I will always accept his coffee. "Do you really think people will show up? I haven't even seen anything on social media."

Koa winks. "Eva said she has it sorted. Let's trust her."

I stifle a groan. "It's hard, you know."

He nods. "I know, Wife. It's hard to rely on others. But I promise, there are a lot of people coming to the bar tonight." He steps back and studies me. "You look nice."

I fiddle with the earrings he made me. He, Cash, AJ, and Teddy have started lurking around businesses near the bar during Foof meetings so they're close by to drive everyone home. They've made candles, custom massage oil, and now silver teardrop earrings. I love thinking of his huge hands manipulating the delicate metal, forming the ethereal jewelry.

"Thank you." I stretch to kiss the tip of his nose. "I love my earrings."

He pinches my backside, making me wish we had time to explore that further. "We are doing a sewing class next. Shall I make you a nightie?"

I shake my head. "Do not say nightie. That's what old ladies say."

"You're my old lady, are you not?" He smacks a wet kiss on my cheek and waves. "I have business to attend to. But I will see you at the bar later, pet."

I watch him leave, marveling at how I made room for him in my life. In my home. And it wasn't as hard as I thought it would be. It wasn't hard at all, actually. It felt as natural as breathing. Things have always been that way with Koa, from the night we met. It just took me a bit to admit it was something special.

I check the clock on the wall above the stove and down the rest of my coffee. I need to get to the bar.

The past three months have been a near constant game of logistics. Koa was right about the fire repair people. They handled everything, but I needed to look at samples and re-approve all the finishes. Instead of hanging wallpaper my damn self like I did the first time, I just had to sign off on the velvet-patterned replacements, and insurance handled all the rest. But then I also had to trust other people to treat my bar with care.

The result looks amazing. We've been allowed back inside for about a week, and today is the grand re-opening. I won't lie. I'm nervous as hell about it. The assholes next door were evicted, thankfully, but I'm still anxious about other people's carelessness. Koa keeps reminding me that we have insurance. We have money. And we have each other.

I should remember that last part most of all.

I park behind the bar and walk inside, expecting it to be empty apart from my sister and Ruthie, who I've promoted to manager. She was thrilled about the extra salary and ... I've been sort of enjoying a few days off now and then. Even if I do spend them at the stadium, watching my husband coach.

I walk down the hall to the bar and freeze in my tracks.

The place is packed. Everyone from Foof and all their partners and kids. All the Brady ladies and their partners and kids. Hell, even the Stag family is here. And Ben, the city inspector.

"What the hell?"

"SURPRISE!" Samantha and Piper clap their hands, jumping a little as they point up at a banner hung from the light fixtures. "It's a wedding reception!"

"A what?" I cling to the edge of the bar for stability, hoping I misheard them.

Chloe shoves a plate of cake at me and grins. "There's cake, Esther. Nobody can be angry if there's cake. Take a bite."

She shoves a fork at my mouth, and I open. It's delicious —lemon cake with... "Is dis lavender?" I speak with my mouth full, overcome with the surprise and the flavors and everything at once.

Koa appears, holding a tray of drinks, wearing a huge grin. He sets the tray on the bar. "Surprise, Love."

"I hate surprises."

He wraps his arms around me. "We know. This will be the last one, honest."

Juniper Jones clears her throat to the side, smiling. "I just have a tiny correction and one small additional surprise. Boys, cut it out!" She hollers at her four sons, who are poised to throw cake at one another. Then Juniper reaches into her jeans pocket and pulls out an envelope. "Expedited, signed, and hand delivered to Mr. Koa Stewart."

He arches a brow and rips open the envelope, then

beams. "Hey. Look at this!" He shows me the plastic card with his face on it. "Permanent resident."

"Oh, babe." I place a hand on his chest, feeling a swell of emotion. I knew this was coming, have known it since the day of the fire. But there's something about having the card, about knowing that Koa is not going anywhere. Ever.

"Good thing we already have a party set up, eh?"

I stretch up to kiss him and feel a surge of want as he licks frosting from the corner of my mouth. Sam pokes me in the arm. "There's time for that later." Koa sighs and releases me, shaking his head. Sam continues, asking, "Koa, I believe we were promised special drinks?"

He grins and relocates the tray of glasses he'd been carrying. "Ah, yes, my masterpiece."

"What's this?"

I'm usually the one who makes the cocktails. Not usually. Always. It's my thing. This is my bar. I don't like that they steamrolled my grand opening and turned it into a wedding party, but I really don't like that they made cocktails without me.

"This is a special one," Koa explains as the noise in the room dies down. "A Pittsburgh twist on a Kiwi treat. Not just a Pittsburgh twist, actually. But a Stormy Hokey Pokey."

My sisters whoop and clap as Koa hands me a glass. "Honey bourbon from Eden's bees and a bit of maple syrup from Eva. Cream from Eliza's goats as well. And bitters."

"Obviously." I sniff the glass. "It smells very sweet."

Koa beams. "Like you, my Love. Truly. I know you're prickly, but I know you have a gooey heart in there."

All my friends unleash a chorus of "aaahs," and I tip the glass in my mouth to drown out the attention. "Oh, wow, Koa."

"You like it?" He rubs my arm, really concerned with my opinion of the sweet, creamy drink.

"It's perfect."

The room erupts in cheers, and my sisters start passing round glasses of Koa's custom cocktail. "When did you do all this? How did I not know?"

He winks. "I've been working at your sisters' places while you've been working like a busy bee." He turns to face the room at large. "Can everyone raise a glass?"

The chatter stops, and even the Stag boys stop running around to listen as Koa talks. I cling to my glass, certain he's about to say something emotional that will make me uncomfortable. "I want to toast my wife, the most amazing woman I know." My cheeks redden as he catches my eye. "Esther, you've shown me loyalty, you've shown me family."

He chokes up a bit, and I instinctively reach for his arm. He smiles. "I was adrift for a long time, Esther, and I wasn't expecting you, but you've given me roots. And now..." He wipes a tear from his eye, and I feel one crawling down my own face. How does he always cut to the quick of a situation? He shakes his head. "Now I can grow where I'm planted, Esther Storm. Like a fern."

Koa turns to the crowd. "Not sure if you all know, the fern is very important to Māori people. The fern is enduring and stubborn. A bit like my wife." He grins. Everyone laughs.

"A bit like you," I retort.

"To Esther Storm, the only silver fern I need. Cheers, love."

EPILOGUE: KOA

"I thought you'd never get home, my treasure." I scoot over from her side of the bed, where I evidently fell asleep waiting for her to get home.

She sinks onto the mattress and groans as she pulls off her shoes. "We had an entire softball team come in near closing. They needed a lot of special drinks."

"That sounds awful." I manage to sit up and start massaging her shoulders as she throws her boot across the room.

"It was fine. Mmm this is nice."

She reaches up and squeezes my hand where it rests on her neck and then spins around so we're facing one another. "Tell me again that I'll survive the flight."

I kiss her. "You'll be grand on the flight." Esther agreed to leave the bar in Ruthie's care for a fortnight, so she can come with me to New Zealand for New Year's. I've spent a lot of time working on my feelings about Aotearoa, about my parents, about how I want Esther to know these parts of me. It's like a dream or a fairytale to have her at my side for this trip. "I promise the hardest part will be the visa paper-work." I kiss her again and help lower her down as she lies on her back in the dim light.

"I just don't understand why we can't travel as our own nationalities. You be Kiwi, and I'll be American, and nobody has to submit bank statements."

Esther runs a finger along my chest, where I've decided I'll get Tā Moko once I'm back on my native soil. Once I can do it properly.

"Mm the only problem is that we'd have to separate in the customs line. And I can't bear to be apart from you."

"You were just apart from me for ten hours, Koa." She closes her eyes, forgetting that she's still wearing her jeans. I start to help her with that problem, and her mouth forms a tiny "oh," of surprise.

"It was torture."

"Yeah, yeah. Oh. Hey." Esther sits up, eyes open, and brushes her hair back from her face. "What do you know about this trip? Samantha is being weird. Are you plotting something with her?"

"I wouldn't dream of it." It's only a partial lie. I'm plotting with Samantha's admin. "She and Lyra told us they have business down under, remember?"

Esther frowns at me. "Sure. And Chloe just happens to be writing a book about colonizers and taking her narrator along to study local accents."

I shrug. "She was very inspired by my perspective on Captain Cook."

Esther pats my hand. "Yes, we all know how she gets inspired."

"I could get inspired." Shamelessly, I drag her hand down toward my crotch, but she growls and yanks her hand back.

"I just want you to tell me if Foof is up to shenanigans. Is this trip to New Zealand going to be a shit-show?"

I hold my palm toward the ceiling. "I swear to you, it will not be a shit-show."

"You're terrible."

"You're no fun. But I love you anyway." I tackle her to the mattress, loving the sound of her laughter until Eva bangs on the ceiling begging us to stop.

Breathless, Esther stares at me. She whispers, "Ka aroha ahau ki a koe."

I stare at her, and her face falls. "Did I mess it up? I looked online. I wanted to surprise you and say I love you in Māori, and I probably messed it up and—"

I press a kiss to her mouth, interrupting her flow of misplaced apologies. "Esther," I whisper. "To hear you say those words, in my first language." I tap my chest with my knuckles. "You don't know how much that means. I love you even more now, tau."

She beams. "That's spouse. I learned that one, too!"

I silence her again with a kiss. And another. I reach for the hem of her shirt, when she nudges me with her chin.

"Okay, so you and I are going to spread your parents' ashes, get you a tattoo, and watch rugby."

"Tā moko. That's correct."

"And Samantha, AJ, and Lyra are going to meet clients, but that has nothing to do with us?"

"Not a thing."

"And Chloe independently decided to write this book and travel exactly right now, bringing her husband along as well as her preferred narrator?"

"And he will probably want to bring his lady-friend for company." I lift the covers, so Esther can snuggle against my side. She might be too tired for hanky panky after work, but she's never too exhausted for me to cradle her in my arms. I pull her tight, feeling the vibrant reality of her. She's prickly and pragmatic, competent and confident, and one thousand percent mine.

I love the feeling that gives me, that I have someone to claim. That I have someone who claims me right back. "It's a shame my sisters can't be there for whatever adventure you have planned, Koa Stewart."

"There will be lots of opportunities for your sisters to come on holiday with us, pet."

She seems to accept the fact that her friends have arranged to all be in New Zealand together, along with their partners. "Koa, I just want to see the ocean and help you get your tattoo. You said the ocean there will be better."

"It'll be the best ocean you ever see. And it'll be warm this time. Remember, it's summer there right now." Esther places an ice-cold foot on my thigh, and I yelp. "I know you're anxious about leaving the bar. But maybe a little less anxious than last time?"

She sighs. "Thank you. It's true. I know I have support if everything goes to shit."

I give her a squeeze and kiss her neck. "You always have me, Esther."

My wife rolls in my arms and cradles my face between her ice-cold hands. I try not to wince because she looks at me so sincerely. "You always have me, too, Koa."

We fall asleep together, planning our trip, planning our future, dreaming of the life we will continue to build. Together.

Thanks for reading Last Call! Want more Esther and Koa? My newsletter subscribers get a wedding night bonus scene.

Visit laineydavis.com to sign up!

If you want to catch the Foof crew from the very beginning, they first show up in my book Vibration: An Accidental Roommates Romance.

AUTHOR'S NOTE

I didn't create Esther Storm on purpose. She showed up when I was trying to create Samantha Vine. If you remember, Samantha showed up in the middle of my Brady Family series. I knew way back at the start of pandemic that I'd make a whole series about a found family of badass women who all hang out in a fictional bar.

And of course, that bar needed a badass owner. Welcome, Esther! Now...she's basically everyone's favorite. Which made it really hard to write her book because I needed to make sure I got her story right.

I really had no idea how much people would love Esther. She's been everyone's big sister. So, I decided to make her a big sister. Her book is all about sisterhood, trusting sisters and taking care of sisters...

I gave her four, and they're each getting a book. The Storm sisters' series will kick off once I wrap up Bridges and Bitters and then try making all the cocktails I've been writing about for two years.

I've treasured the emails and messages from fans who were moved by Foof. There are so many people out there wishing Foof were real...to all of you, I say: let's make it happen. Let's support each other no matter what, fiercely defend each other against injustice, and listen deeply when another woman speaks. We can all release our fucks just like Nicole, Maddie, Elizabeth, Logan, Orla, Celeste, Samantha, Chloe, Piper, and Esther.

But *Last Call* is also very special to me because it's the first time I've written a main character who isn't white or American. I've spent a lot of time the past few years learning about inclusivity in romance, trying to do better about how I identify characters, and making sure everyone feels like they could be reflected in my books.

I always try to make sure I hire someone with a character's unique perspective to read my books and help me portray the characters authentically.

This time, I am incredibly grateful for the wisdom and guidance from Ange Tuulaupua and Te Ata Rikihana, who lent me their expertise in Māori culture. Thank you. Thank you for your guidance as I worked to bring this book to life!

ALSO BY LAINEY DAVIS

Bridges and Bitters series

Fireball: An Enemies to Lovers Romance (Sam and AJ)

Liquid Courage: A Marriage in Crisis Romance (Chloe and Teddy)

Speed Rail: A Single Dad Romance (Piper and Cash)

Last Call: A Marriage of Convenience Romance (Esther and Koa)

Binge the following series in eBook, paperback, or audio!

Brady Family Series

Foundation: A Grouchy Geek Romance (Zack and Nicole)

Suspension: An Opposites Attract Romance (Liam and Maddie)

Inspection: A Silver Fox Romance (Kellen and Elizabeth)

Vibration: An Accidental Roommates Romance (Cal and Logan)

Current: A Secret Baby Romance (Orla and Walt)

Restoration: A Silver Fox Redemption Romance (Mick and Celeste)

Oak Creek Series

The Nerd and the Neighbor (Hunter and Abigail)

The Botanist and the Billionaire (Diana and Asa)

The Midwife and the Money (Archer and Opal)

The Planner and the Player (Fletcher and Thistle)

Stag Brothers Series

Sweet Distraction (Tim and Alice)

Filled Potential (Ty and Juniper)

Fragile Illusion (Thatcher and Emma)

A Stag Family Christmas

Beautiful Game (Hawk and Lucy)

Stone Creek University

Deep in the Pocket: A Football Romance

Hard Edge: A Hockey Romance

Possession: A Football Romance

www.ingramcontent.com/pod-product-compliance
Lightning Source LLC
Chambersburg PA
CBHW030333030726
47499CB00003B/748